Prophesied Kingdom

Titles by J. L. Jackola

Unbound Prophecy Series
Ascension
Descent
Surfacing
Submerged
Riven
Adrift

Unbound Kingdom Trilogy
Severed Kingdom
Cursed Kingdom
Prophesied Kingdom

Prophesied Kingdom

Unbound Kingdom Book Three

J. L. Jackola

Tivshe Publishing

Library of Congress Control Number 2022912735

ISBN 978-1-954175-45-7

Distributed by Tivshe Publishing

Printed in the United States of America

Cover design by Dark Queen Designs

Map design by Worldwyrm

Visit www.tivshepublishing.com

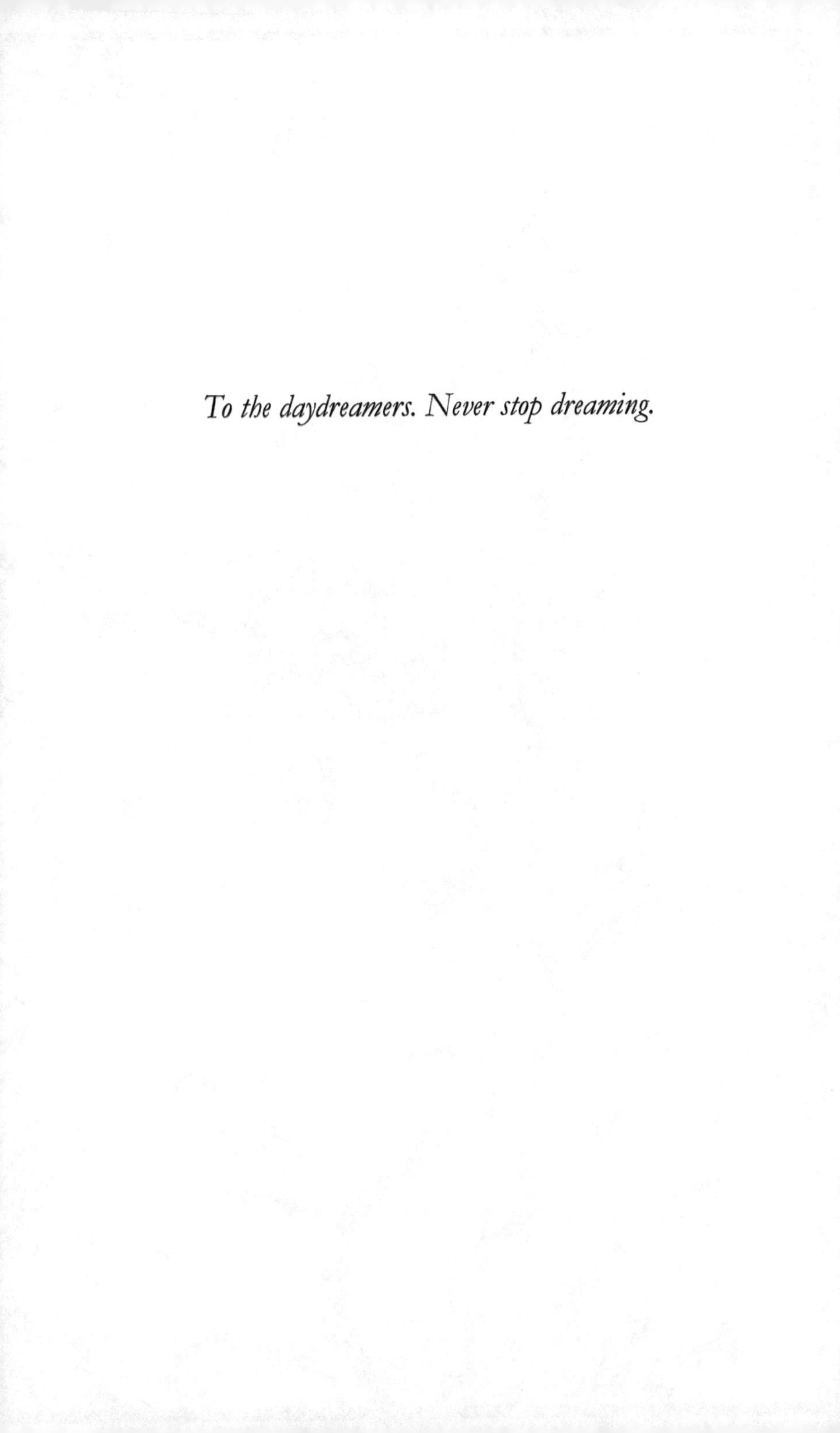

To the daydreamers. Never stop dreaming.

TENEBRON
GAERNEM
western coast

CIRILLA

One

The roaring flames of the fire did little to warm the barren room. Shadows played upon the marble floor, Xali's eyes fixated upon them. Two moons had passed and with them the warm weather that had been expected to last through the warm season. Instead, winter was upon them once again, the sun hidden now behind clouds of black, shrouded for what seemed eternity, taking the warmth with it. As time had passed, the cold had crept in, the snow coming last. What Xali had once watched in wonder, she now cursed for its hinderance.

War had become routine, the Fates and gods battled incessantly, neither side with an advantage, their commotion seeping from the destroyed mountains into Xali's land and Tenebron, the land below suffering, as if their touch clawed the life from it. At times, the fighting was sky bound, other times they pounded the land, sending waves that were felt through every part of the realm. The coastlines were flooded, the churning oceans raging their own wars far beyond the realm.

Xali had lost count of how many days Carnick had been taken from her, unable to bear it, instead choosing to watch the moon cycles. Only one full moon remained, the crack in the larger moon slowly fragmenting it over time.

The hurt, the betrayal still stung, the loss digging talons into the fragments of her heart, the pain tenfold. No one had an explanation, no one had seen it coming, at least that's what they said. But she had. She'd seen the shift in his eyes, the anger that had flared, the struggle she'd ignored, too preoccupied to stop and address it. Now he was gone, an enemy, another monster to fight.

He'd led a ground battle, his army the gods' minions, his power heightened to the level of the immortals. With his betrayal, the family had fractured. It had happened slowly at first, all of them fighting, some blaming Xali for his turn along with everything else. As the angst increased, it had infected them, the subtle signs she'd ignored in Carnick became apparent in each of them as they turned against her. It was an infection she could not cleanse as each lost the battle until the storm clouds in their eyes were cast dark with deep red specks as Carnick's had been. With each betrayal, it became clear that Carnick was recruiting them, calling each to join his army, to fight against her and the Fates, to stand with the gods.

Now only two remained, Mendol and her mother, even fair Fairenth had succumbed, attacking Mendol with a force that had left him in a pool of blood, saved once again by Ren's Lightbearers.

"Xali," Ren's voice pushed through her thoughts. He was standing before the fire, his shadow eclipsing the room.

"Sorry," she said with a sad smile, "lost in thought."

He studied her, his cerulean blue eyes shining even in the shadows.

"Maybe you should get some rest," he said. "Have you slept

since—"

"I'm fine," she replied curtly, cutting him off, not wanting to hear the words spoken aloud again. Each time, it sliced deeper, and she wondered if her heart would ever recover. Since Carnick had left. Since Carnick had betrayed her. Since Carnick had tried to murder her…his wife…the one thing he'd loved above all else. "Really, I'm fine. What were you saying?"

"Your mother and Mendol need to leave," Ren said.

Xali's heart wrenched. "No, they can't—"

"Xali, we agree with him. It's only a matter of time before we turn," Mendol told her.

Xali shook her head adamantly. "No, that won't happen." She looked at the others in the room, the few who were not out fighting: Ren, Paige, the Elvin king, and a handful of others. "It won't happen."

"We can't take the chance," the Elvin king Narilen said. "My people are mortal, as are you. The threat is too strong."

"Xali, he's coming for us next. This is the only safe place left, and if we don't leave now, he'll find it, he'll find you."

They'd taken to the Elvin castle, deep behind the protective tree, the other castles known to Carnick, having now borne the brunt of war. Their people, those who'd sought shelter from the onslaught, hid deep below, each in safety. As each castle had fallen, they'd fled to the only place Carnick had yet to discover, the Elvin safehold. Leaving the people hidden in cavernous dungeons where Xali refused to think on what had occurred in another lifetime. They were safe there, Carnick hunting Xali, beset with a need to kill her, one that drove him to hunt her down like prey.

"I can feel it, Xali, it grows more demanding each day," Mendol said. "The shadows linger within me, their claws scratching at what's left of my resolve. It's only a matter of time before I succumb like the others. Mother feels it, too."

"Even if you leave, he'll find us if you turn. You'll lead him here," she argued.

"No, I can take their memory of this place," Ren said.

She stared at him, not wanting to comprehend the power of that statement. If he had the ability to reach into one's mind and take their memories, could he take the memory of corrupt power from Carnick? Bring him back to her?

As if knowing her thoughts, he shook his head sadly.

"It's best if they go and you remain safe," Narilen stated.

"We will leave at sundown," her mother said, looking at her hands, wringing them in front of her as if by doing so she could take away the oncoming terror that faced her. They'd all witnessed it, the slow change as whatever poison ran through their veins crept its way to their eyes, then their minds, warping their demeanor, tainting it, corrupting it until Xali and all who stood with her were the enemy, bringing Carnick and his army down upon her.

There had been times she'd fought the shift from danger that saved her each time it happened, begging Ren to let her die in hopes that her death would bring an end to it all, but he had refused to listen. They all had, but deep down she knew it was the solution, what the gods demanded.

Would Carnick even mourn her death? The Carnick she knew, the one she'd loved since she was a child, whose impish smile sent her heart leaping, was gone. In his place stood a man consumed by a cursed power, cursed by gods who had stolen him from her. Taken him and turned him, destroying the goodness in him, consuming it with something unstoppable. The shadow of the man she'd loved. Shadows. The word crept through her mind.

"Shadows," she said softly.

"What?"

"Shadows lie in the darkness…just as the gods did," she said, her mind working it out. "They waited there, hidden, locked away by the Fates, we presume. Where did they find the strength to fight, to return?"

"Your aunts saw to that," Ren said.

"Yes, they played their parts, made the sacrifice. Sacrifices of our family, our two heads, and my blood. Only our family. Not random people, not just anyone, but us."

"What are you saying, Xali?" Mendol asked.

"There was a reason. They weren't selected randomly," Ren answered for her.

"No, the strongest, most faithful servants to the gods…" Her mind drifted to the cells where her aunt lay dying, her last words coming back. Xali brought her hand to her mouth, tears welling, threatening to spill. "She was an obedient servant to them even when her cousins bled her to death for their return."

They stared at her.

"Who, Xaliandri?" her mother asked, her voice shaking.

"You know who. She cursed him, she handed his soul to them with each visit to the holy lands, each prayer she taught him to say. Just as it was with every one of them. Our family worshipped the gods arduously, faithfully through every generation, killing those who would question them, killing in their name. Carnick's mother was the purest of them all, an ardent servant of the gods. She saw me as a plague. They all did, an offense to their gods."

"The gods were empowered by your family and brought back with their sacrifice," Ren said, sitting. "By sacrificing you as the last, they were denying the Fates, killing a non-believer in their name."

"One final move to fortify their return. Everyone who worshipped them, claimed by them," she added.

"And you?" he asked.

"Always questioned, never mumbling full prayers," her mother answered, "refusing to go to the holy land for worship even with fear of punishment. We would drag you there each time. From the time you were a little girl, you always wandered from the temple."

"Her voice was always there, calling me away. I never realized until now, but your mother was always there," she said to Ren.

"She called you for the Fates."

"She saved me. And I will be the only one who remains to fight them."

"The key," he said.

Xali stared at the flames. "I don't want to be a key. I don't want to be anything more than who I was."

"And who was that, Xali? A second born in a repressive system built on lies and the backs of the immortals, the blood of their people?" Mendol said.

"Mendol, please," her mother said.

"No, Mother. She needs to wake up. This is happening, Xali. It's been two moons, Carnick is gone, what's left of him is controlling our family, slaughtering our people with his beasts and trying to murder you. You started this, now get your head out of the sand and finish it! Mother and I are leaving. Whether you like it or not, we are leaving. If you refuse to protect yourself, then we'll do it for you. I won't stand by and watch you sulk in your remorse, inviting your demented husband to slaughter you while we watch."

He pulled their mother up. "Let's go, Mother, we've got to pack, and I can't take this anymore." He stormed out, dragging their mother with him, and Xali let them leave.

"He's right, Xali," Ren said, his voice firm. "There's fight in you, but you've let it slip behind your grief. Carnick is out there, and he's claimed everyone you love with the help of the gods. The only thing you can do is fight. Fight to get him back, fight to find the man you love under the darkness. He's there. If my mother was able to pull my father and my uncle, especially my uncle, from it, then so can you."

He put his hand on her shoulder as he left the room, the rest following, leaving her alone with her thoughts, thoughts she didn't want to face.

Xali bid Mendol and her mother farewell the next morning, her mother hugging her so tight it nearly broke her. She looked petrified, and Xali didn't know how to take that fear away. Something frightening was coming for her mother, and no one knew how to stop it.

Mendol took Xali in his arms as he'd done countless times when they were children, the memory of it no comfort, for it stirred memories of Carnick in their youth.

"You need to fight, little sister. Fight for yourself, for us, our people. Fight for Carnick's soul." He brushed her hair back. "They have it, they've claimed it as theirs, but it belongs to you. Take it back and end this. If you truly are the key to this war, then it's up to you."

He kissed her head and pulled way.

"Ready?" Ren asked.

"Yes, as ready as we can be," Mendol replied. "Goodbye, Xali."

Ren shifted them away, leaving her alone in the great hall. He would take them far away and pull the memories of this place from them completely before Carnick had any chance of stealing them when he finally took Mendol and her mother into his fold.

Xali rubbed her arms, a chill settling upon her. She wandered, lost in thought, her feet taking her to the gardens where she'd first met Narilen, her first step in this strange, twisted journey she was now forced to tread. The moonlight lit the space appearing as though magic rays of the Fates themselves leaked through, shimmering upon the plants. She fingered a mauve leaf, thinking back to how lost and confused she'd been then. She'd thought Carnick had betrayed her, thrown her to the family for slaughter. She'd seen the worst in him, so she'd thought, but he'd been innocent, Fairenth having told her mother the secrets that had broken Xali that night. He wasn't innocent this time. An image of his twisted face, lithe with malice rose before her. Hatred burning in his eyes of lava. Gone were the beautiful gray storm clouds that she'd adored, lost were the specks of violet that had shimmered when he smiled. The man she loved was gone, stolen by the gods, a pawn in a war that shouldn't have been.

The bile rose in her throat as it had been doing more frequently as of late, especially when her mind was allowed to wander to Carnick.

"Xali," a soft voice called her name as the bile threatened to spill.

Startled, she turned quickly, too quick to wipe away the tears that had fallen.

"Oh, my dear," Narilen's wife Garnevia said, taking her hand and bringing her in to hold her. "You've been through so much, and none of them are giving you the time to truly grieve. The spirit will only sag with the weight of woe if it is not allowed to be set free of its burden."

The tears spilled. For the first time since Carnick had left, it all came rushing out. There had been no time, no one, not even her mother, to comfort her as the terror had continued. Now, it all came flooding forth. There was no fight left in her, no family left. She was alone.

"Shhh," Garnevia said, soothing her, allowing her the broken moment.

Garnevia held her, rocking her until there was nothing left, until the pain, the hurt, the betrayal had been purged like the tide ebbing.

"Come." Garnevia guided her to sit on the ledge of a section of bright blue flowers happily leaning toward the moonlight, a stark contrast to her own mood.

Xali wiped away the tears, hating the show of weakness.

"Tears are not a weakness. They are the soul's way of cleansing itself. The true weakness is not embracing the feelings that urge the tears forth. Hiding from the pain, the sorrow that your spirit needs to own in order to flourish and carry forth."

Garnevia's green eyes sparkled as she tucked a strand of Xali's hair back, her fingers lingering for a moment.

"You are not alone, child," she said, bringing the strand forth again, its silver shimmering in the moon's light.

"You are a daughter of the Mother Fate as am I. Her blood, her magic runs through your veins as it does mine. We are kin,

Xaliandri, and because of that, you will never be alone."

She tucked the strand back again, her eyes drifting to the fountain across the room, its emerald water splashing rhythmically in the silence.

"Prophecy is a curse to those who must bear it. The Fates do not grant it lightly and so only a few rare chosen ones are part of it. It takes a strength that comes from endless fight, strength only those who have reached the depths of despair, of pain, of abuse can find. The king, Ren, is a result of that fight, his parents' strength to conquer the worst of the Fates' wrath, and so he will not face the pain you do. His parents suffered so that he could be."

Xali held her stomach, the nausea returning as the words struck. "I will suffer as they did?" she asked, tasting the bile as the feel of the creature's claws tore through her again, as the hard unmoving eyes of Carnick's relished her pain.

"Yes," Garnevia said slowly. Xali could feel her eyes on her, watching her struggle. She kept her eyes on the marble, fighting the bile that now filled her mouth.

"You will suffer so that your son may be unfettered by the chains of prophecy."

She lost her fight, and the contents of her earlier meal spilled across the shiny tile. She dropped her head, the lingering taste burning her throat. Lifting her eyes, she met Garnevia's sad green orbs.

"I am so sorry, my dear, but you must now fight for the two of you."

She wiped her mouth with the back of the hand, rising to move away from the mess before she lost control again. "For me and Carnick?"

Garnevia shook her head. "For you and your unborn son."

The world spun as the words crashed down upon her, and Garnevia faded from view, blackness enshrouding Xali.

Two

Xali blinked, the ache in her head challenging that simple task. She tried to sit up, unaware of where she was.

"Careful, move too fast and it won't be a good thing for that head of yours."

She opened her eyes, fighting the sting of the light, making out Paige's face in the blurriness.

"Paige? Where am I? What happened?"

"You passed out, and we brought you here. Ren has yet to return and the Lightbearers are all out either fighting or healing, so we haven't been able to have that nasty cut on the back of your head healed."

She tried to reach back to feel it, but Paige stopped her.

"We've bandaged it as best we could. Someone should be back soon."

"Garnevia, she…" The conversation came tumbling back through the fog in her mind, "…she thinks…" Xali couldn't say the words, the thought too horrifying.

"She thinks you're with child. Yes, it should be an exhilarating thing to discover, but given the circumstances, I'm guessing it's not."

"Something like that."

Paige gave her a sad smile. "Sometimes things we see as burdens are really blessings."

"How can this be a blessing, Paige? I am with child while my husband ravages the lands on the gods' behalf, searching for me so that he can bring my head to them?"

"Well, when you put it like that."

Xali laughed, the action causing a sting of pain in her head. "That's the milder way of putting it," she said, bringing her hand to her forehead.

The door opened, and a figure in what looked like it had once been a white cloak, entered the room. Blood and dirt marred the fabric. He brought his hood down, and Cody's face appeared. He looked worn; soot and mud splotched his face.

"Cody," Paige said, rushing to him.

"I'm fine, Paige, just a little rough around the edges. Your husband gains strength by the day, Xali, and the gods have returned to fighting the Fates. It was quiet for that brief few days, but now they are back. Your husband fights like he is one of them. It's as if he has a shield of their protection around him. We cannot kill him, let alone even harm him."

Xali cringed at his words. She knew how dire the situation had become, but she didn't want Carnick dead.

"Sorry," Cody said. "Garnevia told me I was needed here before I clean up, and it looks like I am."

"I'm fine," she argued. "I've had worse, go clean up and rest."

He came to her anyway, the cool feel of his magic removing the fuzzy ache in her head. His eyes were sad as he brought his hands down, his quick glance to her stomach confirming Garnevia's words. Her heart clenched, and he gave her a sad smile.

"He's healthy," Cody said sadly.

She nodded, knowing to whom he was referring, afraid to speak for fear of breaking.

Squeezing her hand, he said, "Your head will still feel odd for a few hours. You took a hard hit, rest and try not to rise quickly."

"Thank you, Cody," Paige said for her as Xali looked over at the wall, wishing she were alone. Wishing she could take it all back, return it all to where they'd been what seemed ages ago, naïve to the cruelties of the world, to the lies of the once great king. Wishing she had remained blind to the truths that had teased her, turned from them and never answered the call.

"Come on, Paige. I think she needs some space, and Ren returned with me. He'll be looking for you before we return to the battle."

Paige's lips brushed Xali's forehead. "It will be okay Xali," she whispered. "The Fates work in ways none of us ever understand, but they always have their reasons."

As the door closed behind them, a rush of loneliness blanketed Xali. Sitting, she pulled the bandage from her head then brought her knees in tight and let the tears fall. Tears for Carnick, for her father, for the others whom death or darkness had claimed, tears for the unborn child she carried, for her lost innocence, and a youth she once took for granted.

On and on the tears fell until she finally forced them to stop, damning them behind the fragment of strength she still held. Lifting her head, she stared into the dark of the room, the one light orb leaving shadows throughout.

Her eyes fell upon her sword. Carnick had insisted she take it with them when they'd moved temporarily into Ren's castle, before he'd turned. She hadn't seen it since that day. Someone had brought it here, placing it in the corner where it had remained hidden from her view. Had it been there before today? Always shrouded in the shadowy corner of the room? Had she simply been so caught up in her grief that she'd never noticed its presence?

Carefully, she climbed from the bed, ignoring the wooziness that teased within her head. She made her way to the sword, her fingertips hesitantly touching it. Reminders of Carnick came with every touch, his strong arms around her when he had taught her the moves, his voice encouraging her as they'd trained when she'd grown older, the flashes of pride as she'd matured to best even the finest of their guards.

She drew it from its scabbard, the streak of steel echoing in the silence of the room, rekindling something deep within, a hunger, an ember of fight, something she'd lost these last moons.

Pressing her forehead to the blade, she breathed deeply, filling her lungs so that they burned, the flames within growing, the tears turning to anger. The air in the room stirred as she brought the blade down, gripping the hilt tightly, the anger she'd dampened behind the pain cresting until she could hold it no more, a primal scream escaping. Everything that could shattered in the room, shards of glass penetrating the air as her power erupted, falling to the ground as grains of sand as they met her magic, the light orb snuffed out with the force. The black of the room enveloped her, yet the scream continued, running cracks through the walls, splintering the frame of the bed.

As the scream ended, she tipped her head to the ceiling.

"I will bring him home, and I will end this war!" she cried.

Throwing the sword to what remained of the bed, she let the tingle of magic rise, accepting it, not fearing it, opening herself completely to it, both sides of it. She felt the Darkness, the way it danced with her nature magic, enhancing it, morphing it to the magic that made her unique, the power that her ancestors had once held. With it came an awareness of the others who held it. She sensed Ren, the few Darkbearers who were in the castle, the Elvin blood in Ren and the Elvin, a particular calm touch that drew her in. It was and always would be her strongest side. She understood that now, sensed the way the two lines of magic interlocked within her.

Pushing past them, she found the other Darkbearers, then Darkness calling to her in another way, seductive, enticing, it called her Elvin side, the mate of it. She pushed beyond to the tendrils of Darkness that touched her consciousness and found him after she'd sensed her family, each of them, Mendol and her mother, fighting still to not succumb to the foul corrupt power that was hanging over them like a cloak. Past her cousins whose connection to her was slight now that the infected power of the gods had taken over. Her eyes flew open as she touched Carnick, the blanket of foul power turning her stomach, making her want to run, but she didn't pull back as he sensed her presence.

Xaliandri, his voice, unfamiliar, coarse, and twisted flooded her head.

I am coming for you, Carnick.

I look forward to it, Xaliandri. Then I can finally bring your dead body to the gods and end this. This world is theirs.

And you?

Will rule the wastelands with no queen by my side.

You will never rule this world. You will lose, and I will stop you.

His laugh pounded her sensitive head. *And how will you do that, Xaliandri? You are weak, never grasping your full potential.*

I've found it now, and I am coming for you. This will end. I will save you, and if I cannot, then I will kill you myself.

She pulled her connection back, past all the others, touching Ren as she did, sensing his awareness of her until she was alone in her room again. She'd had the urge to shift to Carnick, to end it all right now but knew she wasn't ready. She placed her hand on her stomach, closing her eyes again and accepting the life inside of her, her instinct telling her shifting wasn't an option, she would need to do this the non-magic way.

Tracing her fingers over the loose fabric of the dress she wore, she turned to the wardrobe, still tilted on its side from her awakening. Rummaging through it, passing over the dresses that had been brought to her by the Elvin, the delicate material not what she searched for, until her hand brushed the familiar fabric she wanted. Pushing the dresses aside she grabbed the tunic and trousers she favored, staring momentarily where the fabric had once been shredded by Carnick's beast. It had been mended, the blood that had soaked it cleaned. No longer bearing the scars she knew it once had.

Quickly, she changed, the tightness of her pants around her waist confirming the life she held within her, the loose dresses she'd been wearing concealing it all this time. How many moons had it been since she'd last had a flow? She didn't know, it was always unpredictable, and with the events, she hadn't noticed that it had been absent. How long? Her mind lingered back through the memories of Carnick's touch, the moments of ecstasy they'd shared. It could have been any of them, but it wasn't. In her heart, she knew it had been that first time, that night they'd given in to their need for one another, that night it had all changed moons ago.

The gods had taken her family, her husband, her life, but they would not have her child. She reached for her sword, her resolve returned, even as the words echoed through her mind. *You are the key. This is your prophecy.* It seemed a strange thing to own those words, to finally accept her role in the circumstances that surrounded her. To know that she had the power to turn the tide, she the one who would end the incessant fighting, bring her family back from their insanity, bring Carnick back to her side. She shouldn't have had that power, she was no one, just a second born in a family where second borns were of no need other than for breeding purposes.

But that was the past, all of it lost the day she'd made the first move and awakened the immortals, or perhaps it had been earlier, with her first question, or the first time her mind had wandered from prayers. It was inconsequential now; all that mattered was that this was who she had become, a weapon of sorts, one forced to step into her role, to own it for not only did her life rest upon her shoulders now, but the lives of everyone she loved, the lives of the people of this world, the life of her unborn child.

Shutting the thoughts out, she sheathed the sword and threw the doors to her room open with her power, not looking back at the wounded part of herself she was leaving behind, the warrior having taken over.

Ren waited for Xali. He'd sensed her magic, they'd all felt and heard the scream of anger, power laced as it tore through the castle. Something had changed in her, an awakening, her magic now full and accepted. It was greater than he'd anticipated, and as he'd sensed her brush his mind, he understood that she was now a formidable queen, one he prayed was still on their side. He didn't know if her theory was correct, if she were indeed protected by the Fates, claimed by them while the rest of her family were claimed by the gods, but he prayed that was the case.

There was no question she was special, powerful. It had taken an impetus to call it forth again, she having buried it below her grief over Carnick. That impetus was unfortunate, and he questioned the Fates' actions. Whatever the reason, it had brought her back. Now, he prayed she could sustain it and avoid submerging it below her emotions once again, the Elvin in her risking that possibility. It was the emotional side of her, and he knew she favored it, the Dark the undercurrent to it. She needed the Dark in this moment, to quell the self-pity, the anguish the Elvin in her had been embracing.

The doors to the room flew open before she entered, more magic she hadn't held before. He met her eyes, storm clouds of gray and black furled as lightning streaks of emerald flashed through them. They were mesmerizing. The mix of nature and Dark magic shrouded her aura, the nature taking dominance as they'd thought was the case in her, but the Darkness now present.

"Xali," he said with a lift of his brow.

The others in the room remained tense, and he slipped a protection spell over Paige, feeling Cody do the same over the Elvin king and queen.

"I am leaving. I cannot stay hidden away while Carnick devastates this world with his gods."

"You can't fight the gods, Xali, none of us can."

"No, but I can fight Carnick."

"We haven't been able to touch him, and we're tenfold stronger than you," the Darkbearer Eoin said.

Ren awaited Xali's reaction, evaluating her. There was a gurgle from Eoin as Xali's eyes went still, the green darkening, spreading like moss within them. Eoin struck back at her as the force clamped tighter around his neck. If Ren had been giving the punishment, Eoin would never have dared fight back. The bolt of Dark magic was stopped with a raise of her hand, and the root of the tree from the great hall tore through the doors beside her, ripping half the wall as it slammed into Eoin, avoiding all others and throwing him against the wall. Stone crumbled around him as the thick root sprouted smaller ones that tore through his skin. The weathered Darkbearer he was never flinched, knowing that to do so was a weakness that would bring his king's wrath upon him.

"I think you've made your point," Ren said.

The root receded, Eoin falling to the floor with its release, his wounds healing as he glared at Xali.

Stand down, he told Eoin.

She just attacked me!

She hasn't turned, she was flexing her muscles, teaching you a lesson.

But, sire…

She's fine, Eoin. Be happy she's on our side.

The root stopped before Xali, lovingly running up her arm then through the braid that hung low to her back before it receded completely back to its guarding place.

Ren crossed his arms, watching as the flowers bloomed in her hair where the root had touched, the line of vines marking her bare arms once again as it had when he'd first met her, climbing to her shoulders, flowing beneath her tunic. He still hadn't adjusted to the style of dress Xali wore but it was prominent through her people, and he respected their traditions. Now, he just had to keep Paige from trying to adapt it as she was always looking for a way to escape the dresses his mother had favored.

"So, you're ready to fight," Ren said.

"Yes, and please don't try to stop me. I know it's a risk, but it's my risk to take. This is my mess to clean up, all of it my doing."

"I find that hard to believe. You may have ignited the flame, but the spark was there kindling long before either you or even I was born," Ren said. "I won't stop you, but I will go with you."

"No," she said adamantly. "Carnick is mine. I'll need a horse and some supplies then I'll fight him on my own."

Ren raised his brow again. "A horse? Did you forget your lessons already?"

"I won't shift." She moved her hand protectively over her stomach. "I won't risk it."

Paige had given him the news, a surprising circumstance, one he questioned. Was this a move by the Fates? Was there reason a child would be thrown into this fight? It surprised him that Cody had not been aware when he'd healed her the day of Carnick's attack or that any of them had not noticed after that day, having all healed her with every attack each family member had attempted as they'd turned. It was an easy thing to sense, so why was it hidden from them until now?

"Violissa shifted throughout her pregnancy with Ren," Paige said, addressing Xali's reply.

Ren could see Xali trying to understand how Paige knew such a thing, their history still not known in full to her. He was certain it puzzled her that Paige had known his mother when she'd carried him. They had yet to have time to address the past with her. War had come too suddenly, too painfully.

"I am not the queen. I don't believe I can without harming him."

"She may have a point," Narilen said. "Your mother was immortal as are you, Ren. Xali does not have that protection nor does her child."

Ren sighed; he was right. Xali's mortality was a burden, one that could not be ignored.

"Fine, but you will take Cody and one of my Darkbearers with you."

Xali began to argue with him as did Eoin and Cody. He raised his hand to silence them, Xali the only one who didn't recognize that his command should be heeded or risk punishment.

"It's not necessary," she said. "Your men are needed to fight the army of beasts that roam the lands with the rest of my family."

"You will take protection. A Lightbearer to keep you alive and a Darkbearer to watch your back. You will not sway me on this, Xaliandri, and if I must, I will remind you that my authority outranks whatever resolve you have."

The storm clouds in her eyes came to life again, an angry storm of black rising.

"Do not challenge me on this, Xali, you will lose. You may have found your full power, but mine still eclipses it. You will take them. Carnick is too unstable, and he is protected by the gods. The Fates seem to favor you, but I will not take the chance that we are wrong."

Her eyes calmed, and she gave him a nod.

"I will go as well," Narilen said.

Ren tried to hide his shock. His wife, however, spoke before anyone could.

"No, Narilen, you cannot leave now."

"I must, she is yet untrained. We only scratched the surface when she was first here, Violissa only having a brief time to train her, and now her full powers are present. She will train with me and the Darkbearer the king chooses. Although the Dark guides her powers, the Elvin is the fuel. If she is to break her husband, she must understand it fully."

He was right; they all knew his words held the inconvenient truth.

"But what will I do? What if you are lost to me?"

"You hold a piece of me, Garnevia, and through our children, I will always be here."

"You're with child?" Xali asked.

The Elvin queen nodded. "Blessed with two it would seem."

"Two? Two babes at one time?" Xali asked.

"It is rare," Ren explained, "but not impossible. My mother's mother was a twin as they call it. It is a gift to the Elvin line when it does occur, and those children are often the most powerful of the line, as was my grandmother."

Xali's eyes softened, briefly studying him before turning back to the Elvin queen. "The Fates are restoring the magic of your line to its full potential. Through you both."

Garnevia nodded.

"There is always a means to an end when it comes to the Fates, Xali," Ren said, his mother's words coming back to him.

"So, it would seem. And that's how you knew I was with child?" she asked Garnevia.

"Perhaps. A mother senses these things."

"I can't let you do this, Narilen. You are needed here," Xali said, her tone firmer.

He stood. "I am needed by your side, to fight with you so that the world is still here for the children to be born into. The alternative is not one I wish to dwell upon. The world needs you, just as it did when you stumbled into my realm that night. If not for you, the blooms would not have expanded into the enclave. The fertility, the hope, returned with your presence."

"It is your presence that allowed the babes to be conceived, for they came only when you were here," Garnevia finished for him with a sad smile.

They were right. Narilen had told him how the fertility of the

Elvin had slowed, fewer children born each generation, the very royal line threatened as Garnevia had not conceived in the many centuries they had been married. The Elvin lived extended lives, but their children were never born this late to them.

"You seem to have quite the impact, don't you?" Ren asked. Not waiting for an answer, he continued, "Then it is decided. Narilen, Cody you will accompany Xali on her journey. Eoin, as elder, I will need you to fight by my side, but I ask that you choose another Darkbearer capable of keeping her safe."

Eoin was silent for a moment, then Thane appeared. He wasn't the most recent, chosen to replace Keary when he'd returned to the Fates, but he was still relatively young, chosen only about forty years before the long sleep. He had, however, proven himself on the battlefield, he was sharp, and he was strong.

"Wise choice," he said to Eoin. "Thane will accompany you as well." It was then that a thought occurred to him. "Xali, how do you know where to find him. He's always on the move."

"Not this time, he's waiting for me."

"How do you know this?"

"I spoke with him."

"He was here?" Cody asked, suddenly alert as was everyone in the room.

"No, she found him. Didn't you?" Ren asked, amazed at how her power seemed to have bloomed in such a short time. He glanced to where her hand sat still protectively over her unborn child, the impetus to her final acceptance of her power, her destiny. It had been there all along, beside the fight she'd lost when Carnick had turned on them. And now she had claimed it, along with that spirit, the strength that reminded him so much of his mother.

Ren had felt it, the touch of her presence as her enaigne had slipped past him earlier.

"I did. I found him, spoke with him. He knows I'm coming. He will wait for me so he can bring my dead body to the gods or so he says."

"Enaigne. You have the power of enaigne," Paige said.

"What's enaigne?"

Our ability to talk to one another, Ren replied, *the magic that allows you to hear my voice in your head.*

Xali's eyes grew large. *Carnick has it as well,* she said back to him.

He smiled. *Of course, he does. You both carry Dark blood.*

"Well, this is new and unexpected," Cody said. "Why can't I talk to her?"

"Because you are Light powered, Cody. All the more reason for Thane to accompany you."

"When do we leave, Sire?" Thane asked.

Ren looked to Xali. "I suspect now."

The ground rumbled below Carnick's feet as he looked to the east. Xali was coming to him. She'd been shaded from him, something shielding her from his senses, unlike the others. One by one, he'd found each of them, claiming them, calling that part of their soul they'd pledged to their gods, the souls their ancestors had pledged the day the Fates had abandoned their people. All but her brother and mother who'd been lost to him for some time.

Carnick rolled his neck, the power coursing through him, the power of the gods. They'd taken him, fortifying the Darkness in him, bestowing power like he'd never had upon him. It wasn't Darkness like he knew from his previous life; that had been weak, miniscule. This was a fire that coursed through his veins, Draiol, the gods had whispered to him, their voices burning in his mind as they made him their weapon. The magic of the gods.

He lifted his head, the heat from the scorched ground below his feet empowering him. Mendol and his mother had been hidden from him, but now they had emerged. He could feel the Draiol in them, ready to be turned, ripe for his call. Closing his eyes, he sent his magic forth, claiming it, igniting it, feeling his claws as they met flesh. The mother caved first, weak in resolve, succumbing to his rule, but Mendol fought. He was strong, he'd always been Carnick's rival in strength, no matter that he preferred to keep it hidden in libraries rather than the battlefield. He resisted, and Carnick dug deeper, feeling Mendol's pain.

Yet Mendol continued to fight back.

Do not resist, cousin, for it will only prolong your suffering.

There was no reply as Carnick was the only one who had mastered the ability. Until today. The feel of Xali's voice in his head returned to him, angering him with its gentle, calm strength. His force dug further into Mendol, and he felt his cousin's pain. It urged him on until finally the man caved, and the darkness took him.

Carnick sent his creatures to his new recruits.

You will fight in the east, lay waste to the land, kill any who cross your path.

He searched their minds for any awareness of Xali, any clue as to her whereabouts but found none. Mendol's mind revealed an image of the immortal king.

You will not have her. The king's voice resonated through Mendol's memories.

Carnick roared, the land below his feet bulking, lava spewing. He would wait for Xali to find him, and then he would kill her, just as his gods demanded. He would drag her by her hair then slit her throat, letting her blood spill to allow them freedom. The last piece they needed to escape the mountain range that still held them. The final lock to their prison. His aunts hadn't understood. They'd been wrong, thinking they only needed to bring her blood to the mountain to unleash them. It had woken them but not freed them completely. The Fates had built their prison with layers, and Xali's fresh blood, the sacrifice of her life upon their prison was needed for them to take back their world. When he finally spilled her blood, he would burn her body to ashes as they demanded, far from their sight, her mere presence an affront to their rule. And he knew exactly where he'd burn it, in that unholy site she'd created to cover the essence of the gods. He would take her to the holy lands and desecrate the shrine to the Mother Fate, reclaiming it for his gods.

He looked to the north where two of his gods were keeping the Fates occupied. They would continue to do so until Xali was killed, and then they would destroy the Fates and reclaim the rest of their world. Rubbing his head, he remembered questioning them when he'd first answered their call. Why would they not simply destroy the Fates if they had the power to do so? Why bother with Xali? She was a mere mortal who posed no threat. Or why not kill her themselves?

The only answer he'd received was blinding pain that reached through every corner of his head, the pain unbearable until it had finally stopped.

He'd learned that day not to question them, but a small part of him wondered at her significance. That small part of him that remained, buried beneath the twisted power, the rancid soul whose infection had spread with each day he'd been away from her. It remained locked away, fading with each family member he recruited, with each mortal he killed, with every thought of Xali's impending death.

Three

There was bite to the wind as it whipped Xali's braid at her face. She reached back and tucked it beneath the neck of her cloak, pulling the hood up again to cut the cold. She'd lost track of the seasons, but something told her this should still have been a warm time in their region.

They'd left the safety of the enclave, winding down past the shelled out northern castle of Ren's parents and into a scene that had broken her heart worse than that image had.

Smoke filled the air, the towns lying in ruins, homes trampled, fires still burning. She'd stopped her horse in the deep snow and stared at the open space before her. Gone. It was all gone. Where once proud ancient trees had stood, swaying behind the guardian wall for miles, now stood only barren land. She'd put her hand out as a snowflake fell, only to feel the lack of cold as it landed on her finger and failed to melt. It wasn't snow, but ash. Ash covered the ground below them, not a deep snow as she'd thought.

Tears had burned the back of her throat as she remembered countless hours admiring the beauty of the forests, sketching the giant trees that seemed to almost touch the sky.

"The Sacred Groves have stood since the day our world was created," Cody had said. "They are part of the long history of our world. I'm glad Violissa isn't here to see what's become of them."

"She knows," Xali had answered, turning her eyes northwest where far in the distance speckles of silver and black could be seen dancing in the sky as the Fates and gods waged their war.

They'd kept moving, a slow but steady pace, Cody afraid riding too fast would bring harm to the babe, but Xali knew the truth. He was trying to delay the inevitable. It had been two days, and they'd made it to the Tenebron border. Cody had insisted they stop for the night, and so Thane had built a fire, and Narilen dragged her riding-weary body through training, Thane helping with the Dark side of her newly fortified powers.

Narilen was studying her as Thane directed her.

"I think we're going about this the wrong way. What you did when you stormed into the meeting room was different than what you're doing now," he noted.

"He's right," Thane agreed. "This is small magic that won't come anywhere near what Carnick has."

"That's because she's different than both of you," Cody said, joining them. "She's like Ren and no amount of training from the two of you will help until she recognizes the blend of her power and calls it as one. Only then can she properly segregate it. She must master the combined force in order to master the subtle differences."

"But I thought I did that," she said, blowing a strand of hair from her eyes.

"No, what you did was a result of your emotions; otherwise, you'd be doing it now. Whatever you tapped into that day we left is the fuel for your magic. You just need to find it again."

She gave him a doubtful look.

"Trust me, Ren struggled with the blend of powers he was born with. I was there the day he finally accepted them and mastered them. Now close your eyes and think about what was going through your mind when you last had them."

She looked to Narilen who nodded, then drawing a breath, closed her eyes, relaxing her mind and her body, taking herself back to that moment of the change within her. The strength, the confidence she'd thought she'd lost. In the travel, the emotion of the burned groves, the devastated towns they'd passed, that resolve had diminished. Focusing, she took it back, pulling at her inner strength, the shield she'd worn her entire life, the confidence she'd had each time she wielded her sword. Her fingers grazed the hilt of it, emboldening her and the warmth filled her again.

"There it is," Cody said.

Opening her eyes, she saw the aura around her, an emerald with ribbons of black. She pushed it forth and watched as the land came to life. Leaning into the black ribbons, she touched the Darkness, letting it join with the nature, feeling the volatile force they formed and accepting it, the ground rising and cresting as a hill formed. The wind stirred, the sting of it gone. Instead, it held a warmth she knew came from the Darkness. Pushing her power out, the world came to life, the trees sprouting from their stumps, blossoms filling the fresh grass, the land rising and falling, the clouds overhead dissipating so that the fragmented moonlight danced across her silver hair. With the Darkness, she could push her senses out, feeling the corruption in the air, the taint of Carnick and the others on the land and in their world. She grabbed it and pushed her magic to it, feeling it give and change to a gentle wave that pulsed and crested, calming the air, the aura of the land.

Then she met Carnick's aura. It curdled her stomach, wilting the Elvin in her. She wanted to pull back, to run from it, but the Darkness in her surged forward, empowering the nature, strengthening it, transforming it into something different, something powerful.

Xaliandri, his voice slithered into her head, *I'm waiting for you.*

Good, because I'm coming for you Carnick, she returned. *And I will bring you home.*

He struck out, sending his power through his mind somehow, trying to poison her with it, but she was ready. The Darkness flared at his audacity, striking back with a severity that sent his power sprawling from her mind. She embraced it, let it fill her, feeling its warmth, its protectiveness, and truly understanding the Dark power for the first time. Understanding the Dark king and his Darkbearers, the code they lived by, the protection through force and fear. This was her shield, the weapon behind her Elvin power, the two halves of her a glorious blend of unmatched magic. The Darkness stood guard as Carnick tried to break through again.

She drew back with a confident laugh then stopped, feeling the power he held as it tried to enter her mind again. It was a mix of her own. She sensed the Darkness, the Elvin mutated within it, but there was another power intertwined, a third magic she didn't recognize, its feel heavy and burning, foreign. Under it lie her Carnick. She knew he was there somewhere buried below the manipulative power the gods had layered upon his own.

I will free you from their binds, she said, severing the connection and drawing back quickly before he could reply or strike again.

Opening her eyes, she drew on a breath, not realizing before that she'd failed to do so.

"Thank the Fates," Narilen said.

All three of them were standing at a distance, staring at her. "What?"

"What?" Cody mimicked. "Are you serious?"

"You told me to reach in, and I found it," she said with a smile. "It's amazing. I can feel it like a cloak. I found the Dark, the Elvin, both are one, and it's amazing the way they fit together as if they were meant to be."

"Xali, what did you do?"

"I don't know, I just went back to that moment."

"No, what did you do?" Cody asked, tentatively moving closer to her. He lifted her braid which was no longer braided. In his hands, a thick streak of black lie within the silver. It slowly began to fade, the silver overtaking it again. She met his eyes then let her sight drift beyond where they stood, noticing the field of multicolored flowers, brilliant, lush colors, then the nest of trees that now surrounded them. She stepped back as she took it in, gawking at the now unrecognizable space.

"Did I…" She couldn't finish the question.

They nodded. It was overwhelming, and she was suddenly incredibly weak and lightheaded. Cody grabbed her.

"That's enough for one night or maybe for any night," he said as he gently helped her to the ground.

"I felt him again, but this time closer."

A calming touch of magic swept over her as Cody restored her strength, wiping away the heavy corrupt touch of Carnick's magic.

"Xali, you can't risk speaking with him in enaigne," Cody said.

"I wasn't just speaking to him, I could feel him, his power touched mine. My Dark power surged. I know it now, I can sense it, the beauty of it, the force of it."

"Beauty? Dark power? You must be delirious." Cody smirked.

"She's right, Cody. I could feel her as she accepted it. And you know our power is more than what you see on the surface," Thane argued defiantly. "I felt the pull of her code reacting like something invasive was attacking her."

She shivered at the thought of that third power.

"What was it, Xali?" Narilen asked.

"Something new. It wasn't like either magic that runs through me, it was foreign. From the gods themselves, the antithesis to the power the Fates have given us."

Cody moved back on his heels, almost falling over from the impact of her words.

"Fates, we had our suspicions, but…" Thane paused, a scowl overtaking his features, his brown eyes growing almost black. Xali could sense the call of his power to that Dark part of her. "That's why we can't beat him. Why he can't be stopped, even by Ren."

"A new magic," Narilen mused.

"Or one that was always there," Xali said, her hand moving to her stomach. "Dormant, waiting to be woken. What if it's in all of us? That's the connection, why he claims us all."

"He won't claim you, Xali. You're different, you are a child of the Fates. You said it yourself," Narilen argued.

"But if that power is in me, too—"

"Perhaps it is. Your magic is unique, Xali, and from what you just did, it's strong, on a level with ours or, more likely, close to Ren's," Cody said.

"If he could claim you, he wouldn't be trying to kill you."

She looked at Thane, taking strength from his words.

"That's it," Cody said, "they can't claim you. Something about you is different, aside from how you worshipped. What are we missing?"

She thought back, sifting through the memories, the feeling of always being different, an outcast in her own family.

"Cursed," she said, echoing her uncle's accusation. "They always said I was cursed, my powers never came as everyone else's did, only nature magic, lesser magic and not until I was older. The moons…my uncle always said it was an omen, they all did."

"What about the moons, Xali?" Cody asked.

"They were green, both of them lighting the night sky an emerald green the night I was born."

"I remember that night," Narilen said. "We didn't know what to think of it, the power of it was distinctly Elvin. We all sensed her presence in that moment, knowing it had meaning but never understanding until now." He paused, and Xali waited for his revelation, for some meaning behind what had always marked her as a cursed member of her world. "The Mother Fate. She claimed you before they could. Blessed you, that's why you always felt disconnected to the gods, why Violissa was able to find you. You were blessed, and the others were the cursed ones."

As his words faded, silence ensued, all of them contemplating their power. If it were true, then all she'd gone through, the abuse she'd suffered as a child because of her failings, the struggle she'd had to prove herself worthy of her family's acceptance had been the result of one orchestrated move from the Mother Fate. Everything that made her different, that separated her from the others was the Fates' doing. What else had been their doing? All of it?

A heaviness sat in her chest as she pondered every step that had happened since the day she'd let her curiosity crumble her family's dynasty. Had none of it been her own doing? Her own free will? All of it meant to happen?

"Fates," she muttered. "Our lives were never our own. Mine and Carnick's, always theirs to control, all of this theirs to own, not ours. Is there any free will in our lives or do our lives belong to them?"

It took a few moments before Cody answered her. "Violissa would say our lives belong to them, especially those chosen as part of the prophecy. But, she would also say you have free will. You can choose to turn your back on them, to ignore their call."

"But at a cost," she said.

"Yes, there is always a cost to avoiding their path; however, there is always reward for taking it."

"A lifetime of pain and suffering?"

"Don't judge your path by my sister's."

"How can I not? We're tied too closely now."

"Well, if this isn't a boring conversation. Can we talk about something a bit more uplifting?" Thane complained.

"Uplifting from a Darkbearer?" Cody joked, the tension in the air lifting along with Xali's mood.

They spent the rest of the evening huddled around a fire Narilen had built, filling their bellies with the magical food Thane and Cody created. Xali still couldn't fathom creating food from magic, something in her mind doubting the consistency of it, even though it felt and tasted real, satisfying her hunger each time she ate.

She shook her head thinking of how little her family had known about the immortals and the powers they had possessed.

"Something on your mind, Xali?" Narilen asked.

Smiling, she answered, "No, nothing serious. Just contemplating magical food." She brought the sweet bread up and studied it.

"Ah, I must say it is a gift I envy. If we'd been able to feed and quench the thirst of my people so easily, we would have been happier."

"Instead, you scavenged and hunted?" Thane asked.

"Yes," Narilen replied, "letting the land feed us. Sometimes scurrying over that blasted wall and stealing when necessary. We justified it. Xali's people had stolen our freedom, our lives, we could surely steal some bread."

"All that time, and we never knew your people were there. It still seems strange to me," she said.

"We stayed in the shadows, over time growing adept at being covert and remaining unseen. Only the best trained were sent over the wall. Bringing back food, sometimes trinkets that caught our eyes, but mostly essentials that we could not make ourselves. It wasn't often we went, but it was enough to keep us alive."

"Did you go?" Cody asked.

"When I was younger, before my mother passed and the crown became mine, yes. It was frowned upon of course, I was the heir to the throne, there was much risk involved, or so my parents would lecture me when they discovered my mischief."

They all laughed, and Xali imagined Narilen as a youth, scrambling over the wall, moving in the shadows as he took in life beyond their hidden world. At first, it was a joyful image until she thought about the true reason behind it, the desperate action of a people whose existence had been shattered, whose life as they had known it had been ripped from them. The weight of her ancestors returned to her shoulders, and her mood turned sullen.

"Your Elvin emotions need to be tempered, Xaliandri," Narilen said, sensing her shift.

"He's right," Thane agreed. "It is those emotions that rule you, rule your magic, and they must be controlled, or they will render your ability to fight useless."

"Perhaps," Narilen mused, "or perhaps not. If her emotions are high, her power is impressive. Perhaps the two must be present, the emotion embraced, understood as a catalyst for the Darkness that lies below, the fuel for it to reinforce the nature she holds."

Xali stared at him, contemplating what he'd said, but it was Cody who responded, "Why are the Elvin so confounding? Can you not speak normal? Always so deep and convoluted. Violissa is the same way…was…always spouting random deep thoughts from nowhere."

Xali laughed. "They weren't from nowhere, Cody. And I understood exactly what he meant. The emotion comes from the Elvin side of me?"

"Yes, we are very expressive."

"Sensitive, unstable bunch is what you are," Thane grumbled.

"Says the Darkbearer," Cody teased. "Really Thane, you do need to think about your comments before your mouth opens."

Thane drew his power, and the Darkness coated Xali's skin.

"See, now who's unstable and oversensitive?"

Thane hit Cody with his magic, and Cody was sent tumbling.

"I went soft on you, Cody. Test me again, you may end up with blood on your shiny white cloak."

Cody only laughed as he brushed himself off and walked back over to his seat. "Moody you Darkbearers are, so moody all the time."

Another laugh slipped from Xali even though she was trying hard not to let it free. The playfulness was cut short as a howl was heard in the distance, shattering the silence. It wasn't close, but that didn't mean they weren't in danger.

Cody and Thane rose quickly, Cody dousing the fire with his magic, and both men turning serious once again. Narilen offered her his hand, helping her to her feet. The four stood, listening, a second howl coming only moments later.

"We'd best move. They're not close, but they move swiftly, and I don't want to risk the chance that they'll overtake us."

Cody had grabbed the horses, they gathered up what few things they had, and mounted, ready for another few hours of dauntless riding.

Another howl cut the night followed by a long screech, both sounds still far in the distance. Xali glanced back as they began to ride, unsure whether what lie behind them or before them terrified her worse.

Ren sank into the seat, exhausted from the battle from which he'd just come. The beasts were wicked and strong. It had taken his combined power with Eoin's to take this one down. Yet it seemed for every one they killed, another two took its place. They were like a plague that couldn't be stopped. He leaned on his knees and put his head in his hands.

"Why are you sulking in the corner, Ren? Come to bed, although perhaps you should bath first, you smell quite rancid," Paige's voice called from the bed, the dark of the room enshrouding her.

He laughed. "I thought I was quiet enough to avoid disturbing you."

"I know your worry. It's heavy enough to wake even the dead."

He stared at his hands, knowing she was right but having nothing to say about it. There was nothing to do but worry. The world had fallen to chaos, his people were dying, his men were exhausted, and now Xali had left to face Carnick whose only intent was to see her death at his hands.

"Worrying won't make any of it go away, Ren." He felt her hands on his, having heard her leave the bed.

"No, I don't know that anything will make it go away."

Lifting his hand, he made tiny light spheres above them that sparkled in her blue eyes, catching the highlights of her auburn hair. He brought his hand down to touch her cheek, and she leaned into it.

"Do you still have faith Paige?" he asked her.

"Always. Your parents are up there now. There's no way they would let the other Fates fail. They have too much to lose."

"But what if they aren't enough? What if they do lose?"

"You must be delirious. Your father fought tooth and nail to save your mother countless times. There is no way he would ever lose her now. It's not an option. I pity the god who dares touch her, for they will experience a wrath like no other."

Chuckling, he thought back to the moment the gods had woken, seeing his father's reaction as one of the gods had turned on his mother. Paige was right; his father would let nothing happen to her, plus he had Tynan by his side. Tynan would protect his mother to the death, his father as well. It was a strange thing to think, but it was a sworn oath he had taken upon his redemption.

"You're right." He sat back and looked at her, her smile not quite shielding her own fret but enough to minimize his. "Besides, my mother isn't one to be reckoned with either. You may want to pity the god who does face her. I've dealt with her magic one time too many to doubt her ability to protect herself."

"As I was saying, no need for worry."

He let his fingers drape through her hair, taking comfort in its softness. "Your optimism wins yet again."

She leaned up and kissed him. "It always does."

Then she waved her hand before her face, saying, "You really do need a bath."

Laughing again, he rose, picking her up and tossing her into the bed unceremoniously before heading to the tub room. She let out a surprised squeal as she landed, but he heard her giggle as she crawled back under the covers.

He paused at the doorway, a thought coming to his mind, one he couldn't quite shake. One he'd been keeping below the surface where he couldn't dwell upon it.

"Ren?"

He sighed. "She's going to her death, Paige. It's inevitable."

He heard her shudder, sensed the fear that swept through her, burying the optimism. "Instinct?"

"No, knowledge. I don't know how to explain it, but it's stronger than instinct. This entire thing has been leading to her death, and I can't stop it."

"Maybe you're not meant to. Maybe this is bigger than all of us. Bigger than you."

He turned back to her; the lights he'd made reflected in her eyes still, along with the sadness they now held. "I'm to simply let her die? How do I do that?"

"The same way your father was forced to leave your mother in Tynan's grasp, knowing what it would cost him, what it was costing her."

"A means to an end. Always a means to some end of the Fates' purpose. Do you ever tire of it, Paige? My mother did, and I know for certain my father did."

"I don't think we have a choice."

"We never do, do we?"

He turned from her, knowing there was nothing more to say, that prophecy ruled his life as it had his parents'. That decisions had been made long before any of them had been born, decisions that revoked their own free will, laying a path no sane person would ever tread, yet all of them forced to do so or face a wrath that held consequences far worse than what the path held.

Praying, hoping his parents, the Mother Fate, any of them heard, he stepped through the doorway wondering if his bath could wash away not only the physical burdens of this war, but also the mental ones.

***

Xali and her companions traveled two more days, passing through Tenebron's border on the sixth. The closer they came to their destination, the heavier the air, the colder the sting of the wind as if even it were trying to keep her away.

"We should begin camping during the day, keeping hidden in the shadows as we travel. We've gone unnoticed thus far, but I don't believe we will remain that way," Narilen said.

Cody and Thane agreed, and so they found a lone patch of gnarled trees under which to stop. Cody made food, and water was found for the horses. As Xali chewed the sweet bread he'd created, she marveled once more at how he'd created it from his magic, a thought coming to her.

"If you can do this, why do your people still harvest the land, why not keep them fed?"

"The people need to know how to fend for themselves. We are their protectors, their healers, but they must have will to live for either of those things to matter."

She looked at him curiously.

"If we did all of the work for them, what would that accomplish?" Thane asked. "It would only serve to create a spoiled, expectant people. Besides, we are not slaves to our people. We use our power as needed, not as demanded. The Fates bless us with these gifts not so that we can spend our days catering to the wants of the people but so they can live peacefully, happily without fear—"

"Well at least in the past they did," Cody grumbled.

They fell quiet, the silence strangely comfortable.

"My sister always insisted the people know the land, she would spend her days with them, toiling it until the sun went down," Cody said, reminiscing.

"Your sister, the queen?" she asked, remembering him saying something similar a few other times. Remembering the first time she and Carnick had heard him say it, a time before the madness had stolen him from her.

"Yes. Violissa."

"You never did quite explain that." Her mind went back to the day of punishment. "How can that be? They said we would now bear only one child as the immortals do. If they only bear one child, how can she have a brother? And…the king, he had a brother as well." She'd never realized the brother was a mistruth to those words.

"Well, you see, that's a bit of a long story."

"Make it short, Cody," Thane grumbled.

"Violissa and Sinow are exceptions. It is true, immortals as you call us, have only one child, only the rulers bear children. The rest of us—"

"Denied the pleasure of the flesh," Thane said for him.

Xali found that surprising, but Cody continued, giving her no time to question it.

"There are only a few exceptions to those rules, all made as part of the prophecy. Tynan was a necessary part and so he was born, a second son to a king who had expected only one as every king before him had. The reasoning, the journey he traversed with them too long to conquer at this time, or risk Thane's anger. In short, the Fates created him to drive the prophecy to fruition, and so he became a second son."

"And you?" she asked, vowing to learn all she could about the past of the immortals when this was over, too curious not to.

"A fluke but another piece to their prophecy. I was not born in this world, so by definition and the laws of their nature, I am not Violissa's brother. I was born in another world while she was trapped there, reborn life after life until Sinow saved her. One of those lives included me, her brother. The Fates brought me here when they returned, and I was chosen by the Fates to serve as her Lightbearer."

"Another world, like Chastity?"

"Yes, Chastity is from my world. Her story is an even more convoluted one."

"I'm beginning to sense a theme," she said, laughing, the lightness of the moment relaxing the tension she'd carried these past days.

"Why did you not return to the Fates with them?"

He shrugged. "It wasn't my time. I was the youngest of Violissa's Council. Called just as they took the throne. It made sense for me and Eoin who was called at the same time to stay on as elders. I love my sister and Sinow, despite all that moodiness he broods in, but I also have a nephew. One who is new to the crown, one I adore, and want to see flourish as his parents were eventually allowed to do…well before your great king mucked it all up. I'll stay on and see this out, stay by his side just as I did with Violissa and Sinow."

Xali looked to the fire they had lit, its flames dancing in the breeze. "I'm glad you stayed," she said softly, thinking of the impact he'd already made on her life.

"Maybe it was meant to be," he said, "the Fates lead us in ways we don't always see until after we've traveled their path."

"And do you think that's the case now? That everything we're going through has an end purpose, that we'll understand it once we've followed the path's course?"

His blue eyes sparkled in the light of the flames. "My sister was a firm believer in the Fates, trusting them after her initial misstep. She never wavered after that, and they threw everything at her, pain, trauma, loss, they ripped her from Sinow countless times, and through it all, she remained faithful to them, knowing that there was a reason, that she and Sinow would find their way to the prophecy's end."

"And you?"

His eyes grew sad. "They found their way, they were finally happy, blessed by the Fates and chosen to walk among them."

"You didn't answer the question," she pushed.

He gave her a small smile. "I remain faithful to the Fates, I believe in them, that they have their reasons, just as Violissa believed.

But as with Sinow, I question their means of getting there, question the methods as well as the intent."

"Their intent?"

"They were chosen to be Fates, the three of them but did they finally get to rest? Finally experience the unfettered life they struggled to find in their lives here? They're up there, fighting the gods, weapons of the Fates. So, it does lead me to question if blessing them to stand with the Fates was truly a reward or another means to an end."

"Weapons to fight a war."

"Aye, left again without the peace they deserve."

He dropped his eyes, a silence coming over them, no one truly knowing what else to say. Xali stared at the remains of her sweet bread, pondering Cody's words. Was there no end to it? The king and queen had fought for eons longer than she, and still they were tools of the Fates, their happy ending not yet attained. What did that mean for Xali and Carnick? Would she die at his hands as she suspected she would? Her life taken in a war that was never hers to own but was now her burden to end.

Four

Carnick jumped from the catlike beast, landing firmly on the rocky terrain. He gave the beast a pat, its abrasive fur tearing at his skin as he did so. It loped away to curl into the corner of the cave below where Carnick had created his throne room. He knew as it settled, it would blend into the surface, returning to the molten rock from which the gods had formed it, waiting to be called to duty once more.

He walked to the mountain edge that lined his dwelling, having carved out his own palace within the shelled remains of this part of the mountain when the gods had called him. He was close enough for them to speak with him, but still far enough below their battle with the Fates to avoid dealing with their mess. At first, he'd thought the Fates would flush him out, kill him for harming their new chosen one, but to his surprise, they'd let him be. Perhaps the gods had known this would be the case, known he too served a purpose and so the Fates would leave him to his own destiny.

Destiny. He laughed to himself, thinking on how the immortals had only considered Xali in their grand scheme, never thinking he was worth any notice. The immortals and their damned Fates. All the while, the gods had been calling him. He hadn't noticed, other than a few moments, until they'd awoken. Blinding himself to their call, he'd ignored it, trying to stay true to Xali, to the belief that she was the one who held importance. But with time, their call had been too strong, so strong that it had drowned all that Carnick had been, submerging even the love he'd once held for her.

Growling, he rubbed his hands through his hair, forcing the thoughts away. He'd allowed her to take the lead too often, let her push him to the side, making him the second born. No longer. He was stronger now, his mind not muddled with confused thoughts of love. Now, he had a purpose, he had the gods, and they would reward him for giving up the life of soft-heartedness he'd held.

For a fleeting moment, a memory of innocence flitted through his head. Xali with her silver hair and stormy eyes, the flecks of emerald glinting in the sun as they stood in the holy land in their youth. The memory of how his heart had filled when her eyes had met his, even though they were meant to be closed in prayer, threatened to unleash something that lay far within him.

He squeezed his hands so tight that blood leaked from them, then spit on the ground as if doing so would cleanse his mind of the thought. Instead, he thought of the holy land they'd been standing in. The land dedicated to their gods, one she had desecrated, she and that blasted queen. She should have been praying that day, rather than seducing his heart, stealing him from his purpose, from worshipping the true gods. She was a sacrilege to their gods, a worshiper of false deities, and she would be punished for it.

The holy lands were tainted now with the feel of her and her damned Fates. The immortals had seen to it that everything he and their family had held dear was removed. Carnick had gone to the site of his home, the palace where he'd been raised, one that had held so many memories. It had angered him that they'd obliviated it, erased it from existence as they had his family, as the Fates had his gods. In his anger, he'd scorched the ground, wiping away the touch of them, the feel of their magic and that of their Fates. He would erase them from existence just as they had his family. Make them pay for all they'd done right after he killed Xali and freed his gods.

As his attention turned from his thoughts, he heard the rush of wings, the winged viper Sartria favored landing behind him. He heard her dismount, sending the beast to its slumber.

"Cousin," she said seductively, coming behind him, her hands touching his back. He flinched, it felt wrong, she felt wrong. "She comes. Just through the border of your province."

"I have no province. She took that from me."

"Ah but you will have the world when she is dead." Her whisper was too close to his ear, and he turned to find her dangerously close.

The storm clouds in her eyes raced with red lightning bolts, stirred by some desire that did not match his own.

"You will need a queen to rule by your side, Carnick," she said, her hands skimming his chest.

He eyed her, weary of her attempts at a throne he had yet to hold. Just as it had been in their youth, she never tired of her seductions. Now, it had become more flagrant, her total disregard for her own husband not going unnoticed. The call of the gods spoke differently in each of them, enhancing what qualities they'd had prior. She had always been a seductress, and with the change, that had only worsened. Her clothes were worn tighter, her necklines lower. She'd even taken to enticing the men of towns they would attack, stealing a few for her own pleasure before killing them.

"Leave me be, Sartria. You're not getting my throne."

"I don't want your throne, Carnick. I want to share it with you, just as I want to share your bed, as I always have. I've never kept that a secret. You are the strongest, the one who holds the greatest power in our family, you always have been." She pushed her body against his, but her words poisoned her movement.

Shoving her away, he backhanded her. "Keep your hands off me. I will never be yours nor have I ever wanted to be."

"Don't tell me *she* still holds your heart," she hissed, her eyes darkening.

He grabbed her by the neck and squeezed until he heard the air stop. "She holds nothing just as you do." He threw her to the side. "Now leave me be or you will die by my hands before she does."

He turned his back on her and stared angrily out at the broken land before him, waiting until he heard her scurry away before relaxing. Rolling his neck, he thought about her words. He would need a queen, but she turned his stomach, her latest deeds turning him completely from her. She and Ainia were the only matches available, however. He would have to take one of them eventually, regardless of the fact that they'd been joined already. He would be king; it would be his right to take who he wanted to the throne. Fortunately, he didn't need anyone by his side now and had chosen to defer that decision until after the war was won. Until then, he would have to put up with Sartria's incessant nagging. If she annoyed him enough, he would simply kill her and take Ainia. It made no difference to him, as long as the bloodline stayed pure.

A chunk of stone fell from above, piercing the ground next to him. He didn't flinch, knowing he was protected. The gods needed him alive. He focused his eyes back to the distance, deferring thoughts of the future to another time. The only thing that mattered now was Xali. Clenching and unclenching his hands, he waited, watching patiently for her appearance, knowing that when she finally did arrive, the true battle would begin.

Xali, Narilen, Cody, and Thane broke camp that night, riding another two days. The closer Xali drew to Carnick, the stronger she could feel her connection to him. She knew when he left the desolate mountains, knew when he returned, never once bothering to seek her out, to fight her, waiting for her to reach him, to face him in his territory, with the gods standing as witness. Would the Fates stop them, or would they all bear witness to her impending death?

She hadn't told anyone, but she could feel it coming. The long ride her final, leading her to whatever part she would play in the prophecy, to her destiny.

"Shame we don't have the Stiorme," Narilen said.

"The what?" she asked, putting her thoughts aside.

"The Stiorme," he replied. "Majestic horse-like creatures that walk the Elvin forests. They are swift and can travel three times the speed of these horses."

"We rode one…Carnick and I when we first came upon the enclave," she said, remembering the night it had found them in the forest. Carnick's name was as lead upon her tongue as she said it.

"They once roamed free within the enclave and through the Sacred Groves, but they were slaughtered to mere numbers when your ancestor seized the land. We saved a few and when that obscene wall had been up long enough, we slowly let them wander but never further than the valley."

"Except for this one," she said, "he found us deep in the woods."

"Fates at work once again," he muttered.

They fell silent, the moons lighting their path until she asked the question she'd had on her mind since she'd first heard the term.

"What are the Sacred Groves?" she asked as they came to a clearing, skimming the edge of the treeline for cover.

"The forests that run from northern Cirlillia through northern Tenebron. You would have seen them in the distance."

She looked beyond the open space to the north, but only open land lay far beyond. Something nudged at her memory, but the terrain looked no different.

"The Groves are thought to have been the birthplace of the races. Once they were thought to be the place where the prophecy of Violissa and Sinow was created, but that was not the case. They have seen much, survived through millennia of strife, war, and devastation. Always, they survived."

"Until now," Cody said wearily.

Xali remembered leaving through the snowlike ash, miles of it layering the land.

"He burned it."

"It was an affront to the Fates, a call of war, one of his first acts when the gods armed him. They burned for days, the Mother Fate too distracted to stop him."

"She couldn't," Xali said. "The war on ground is ours, the Fates can only fight the gods, we are left to fight each other."

"You see as an Elvin would, as my sister did. Beyond the sight of mere mortals. Listen well to it, for it will guide you while the rest remain blind," Cody told her.

He urged his horse forward, catching up with Thane, and leaving her to her thoughts. She stared at the open field to her right, a layer of black covering its barren terrain. She slowed her horse and directed it closer, the familiarity of the land calling her.

"Xali, stay to the tree line and with us," Thane commanded, but she ignored him, dismounting her horse.

As her feet hit the coarse, charred ground, the memories flooded back.

"Xali, that's not wise," she heard Cody say.

She walked forward, memories of her youth filling her vision. Of Carnick's gentle touch, the strength of his presence, the playful winks and coy smiles. This had been his palace, the place he had been raised, one she had spent countless time in, gone now. She'd known the immortals had removed the family palaces, but she'd been told they'd been replaced with land, fertile and blossoming. This wasn't the work of the immortals. She touched her hand to the ground, feeling Carnick's power, the force of it charring what had stood there, burning it so far down that even the dirt below was blackened. His anger at the absence of his history, his heritage, climbing still from the ash.

"They really did erase us, didn't they?" she whispered.

She heard them dismount, heard the footsteps grow near, the hooves of the horses as they were pulled to be tethered before Cody came beside her.

"You erased us from your world, like we never existed?" she asked him.

"Isn't that what your people did to us?" he replied, his words tearing at her soul.

She felt the pressure of the tears but forced them back.

"We gave you more than you gave us or our people, but we did take back what was ours."

She nodded, knowing he was right.

"A town stood here once. It was a small village, but it was a village just the same. One with families, children who played on the very spot our feet stand. They were erased from your history as well, but not from ours. Violissa created a beautiful field of minth, flowers that never fade, insisting it would forever mark this space in their memory. And once again, your family has stripped that memory, discontent to recognize any existence but their own."

"Carnick," she said softly. "This was his home, his palace that stood here."

"Well, I guess we pissed him off then, didn't we?" He turned and walked away. "Don't tarry long, Xali. It's not safe out here."

She looked back at him. His head was hung low, his usual proud stance heavy with the emotion he carried.

Thane and Narilen wore expressions that mirrored his. What had Drakine done to all of them? His scars ran deep, and she wondered if they would ever heal.

"For what it's worth, I'm sorry. For everything he did to you and your family. I'm trying to make it right, I've been trying for forever, but I don't know that I ever can."

Cody stopped. "Even the deepest scars can be healed, but it takes time, centuries, even more sometimes."

"But they will heal," Narilen said with a smile. "Thanks to you, Xali, we have the chance to do so."

She mouthed a small thank you and turned back to the space, prepared to say her goodbyes to a past that could no longer be.

A flurry of wind hit her, ash moving to blind her. She heard Thane shout as a vicious roar cut the silence. A beast tore from the tree line, but Xali's attention was drawn to the winged viper that landed before her, her cousin Sartria upon it.

Xali drew her power, Thane shifting next to her. She heard Cody and Narilen fighting behind them. Sartria slid down the beast, landing with a force that shook the charred ground. How had she become so strong?

"Well, well, little cousin."

Xali felt Thane's magic wrap around her, a protection spell. The tail of the creature pulled back ready to strike.

"It's been a while, little cousin. You look tired but don't worry, you won't be alive much longer. Then you can sleep for eternity."

Something struck Thane unexpectedly from behind, and the viper's tail jutted out at him as he balanced himself. He was thrown but shifted back, the creature striking again, Thane forced to fight it.

"That takes care of all your soldiers, cousin," Ainia said, bringing her own beast to a halt and sliding down it to join Sartria. The beast's red eyes glared at Xali. "You can't kill her, Sartria, remember Carnick wants her. He wants to crush her soul and feed it to the gods."

"That doesn't mean we can't have a little fun first."

Xali dared a glance behind her and found Narilen and Cody fighting a massive catlike creature, its tail dragging Cody each time he tried to make it to Xali, their magic filling the air, hues of blue and black from Cody and Thane, who was still fighting the viper-like creature. Around Narilen, the world was a haze of green vines and roots climbing over the beast's paws.

A hand grabbed her face. "I need your attention on me, Xaliandri. You are coming with us. It's time we put the traitor down like the dog she is."

Sartria grabbed her hair and yanked Xali forward. The world seemed to slow as the anger built in her. She pushed Sartria back with her power as Ainia buckled the ground below. Xali stilled it then sent it rolling back beneath her so that she was thrown with her cousin.

Xali's power coursed through her, the wind wrapping her hair around, awaiting her command.

"I see you've learned a few tricks," Sartria said. "Well, they won't be enough. The gods want this world, Xaliandri, and they will take it back. Carnick will sacrifice you to give them back what is theirs, and nothing you do will stop him."

Sartria threw herself at Xali, toppling her before she could react, clawing her face and pulling her hair. It was a physical attack she hadn't expected, and her power waned as she was put on the defensive. For a moment, she was lost until Ainia joined the fight, kicking her in the stomach.

The baby. Years of battle training came back to her. She grabbed Ainia's foot as it came down again and ignoring Sartria's attack, twisted so that Ainia fell hard to the ground.

Then she punched Sartria hard enough to stun her, bringing her knees up to throw her from her body. Xali jumped up in one quick move, ready to fight, drawing her sword.

"You forget, while you two were bathing in scented oils, I was training for battle." She spat a mouthful of blood out then wiped her mouth with the back of her hand.

The four-legged beast shrieked as Cody and Narilen finally took it down. Cody, shifting to her side.

"Go back and tell Carnick I'm coming for him. I will free you all, Sartria."

"What makes you think we want to be freed? Carnick is king

now, cousin, the king he should have been, and we will rule beside him. Once this is done, and your blood is spilled, I will take your place in his bed, cousin, and I will show him what true pleasure is."

Xali slapped her, drawing blood.

"You haven't won, Xaliandri," Ainia said as Sartria continued to glare at her, her hand to her cheek. "You will lose, starting today." Her eyes glanced back, filling with black storms, and Xali turned too late as the creature Ainia had ridden slashed Narilen, its claws shredding through his body in one fierce swipe. A blast of Dark magic ripped the beast from Narilen, as a mist of arcane flew to him, but Xali could see the haze in Narilen's eyes as he fell, the blood seeping through the front of his shirt where the claws had gone straight through.

Xali screamed, her power overflowing, power she aimed at Ainia. Her sword pulled from her hands and impaled Ainia, thick vines erupted from the ground, piercing her throughout her body. Her eyes remained wide with shock as death took her.

Sartria stumbled back and called the other creature as Cody ran to Narilen, Thane remaining at her side.

"Crawl back to your king, Sartria, and tell him I'm coming for him. And know this, I will not hesitate to kill anyone who threatens my friends, family or not."

Sartria climbed the viperlike creature quickly.

"Oh, and Sartria, you dare touch Carnick, and I will ensure your death is slow and pleasurable to watch."

The beast rose in the air and took Sartria away as Xali ran to Narilen. Blood was seeping from his mouth and everywhere she looked, his skin paled against the vibrant red of it.

"Cody, why isn't he healed? Do your thing and make him better like you did for me," she pleaded.

Cody shook his head sadly, but Thane answered for him. "They can only heal those who have yet to be claimed by the Fates. It's too late."

Xali was stunned. There were limitations to healing? "No, no, that can't be. Cody, please heal him."

"I can't," he answered sadly. "The wound went straight through, it was fatal. The most I can do is make him comfortable until the Fates take him. It is against our powers to steal a soul from the Fates once they have claimed it, it cannot be done, even if I tried."

Narilen's hand grabbed hers, pulling her close, his green eyes faded now, their brilliance replaced with a deep sage. He placed something in her hand.

"Take it to Garnevia," he gurgled. "For our children. They will exist because of you, Xali. Never forget that or doubt your place in this world. Before you, Garnevia was barren. You have blessed us to live once again."

He squeezed her hand as her tears fell then his sight drifted beyond her. A warmth filled the air, and a calm settled upon her, a golden glow surrounding them before it faded with the warmth.

Narilen's chest rattled as his last breath faded, his eyes staring blankly until Cody gently closed them. They stayed there, huddled around his body until Thane woke them from their state, insisting they move on. They burnt Narilen's body, Xali knowing they would be left alone now, Carnick having suffered a blow to his army with the loss of Ainia. As the flames died, Cody said a prayer, Xali finally opening her hand to look at what Narilen had given her. She ran her fingers over the engravings on the white stone.

"It is Elvin, the necklace worn by every Elvin king or queen since our creation. You will bear it to Narilen's wife who will ensure his firstborn child wears it as he and those who came before him have."

"He didn't even get to see his unborn children, or tell Garnevia goodbye, that he loves her one last time."

"She knows," Thane said. "The Elvin know, and she is grieving his death as we speak, their tie beyond our understanding."

They fell silent as they moved to her cousin's body, debating what to do. Xali stooped beside her, brushing her silver hair back.

"She was a good person at heart. They all were. It's not fair that deeds of generations before us have cost her her soul," Xali said. "We used to play together in the fields of Old Tenebron. She was older than I, they all were, yet she treated me no younger. She would let me dress in her gowns long before I fit in them, take the berries and stain my lips as hers were stained. I stood by her at her joining." The tears fell again, too many spilled this day. "It's not fair, none of this is."

She felt the warmth again as it caressed her skin, that calming feel that caused her to look up. The queen stood before her, a sliver mist around her. She looked to the others, but they were frozen as was everything else.

"It isn't fair, but then no one ever said it would be, child," the queen said softly.

"Are you here to take her soul?" Xali said, hoping her fears were wrong.

"No, her soul has already been claimed. The gods own her as they do all of your family now."

Xali's heart burned with her words.

"Even your husband."

"They're all lost?"

The queen's emerald eyes shimmered with a gold sparkle. "Perhaps not all, some yes, but not all."

Ainia had been lost, the others lost before the war, before the terror, her father and Carnick's mother, their uncle. Her aunt, maybe both aunts? Lost to the very beasts they'd raised. Is that why Ren had been unable to sense them? She felt no grief, they had tried to kill her, had succeeded in killing her father. Pity was what came to her for the senseless loss of their lives as well as all the others. It was on their shoulders that Ainia's death lie.

"Your path is a hard one, Xaliandri. One which I more than anyone else understand."

"And there is no turning back," Xali said, the resolve returning to her.

"No, there is not." Her eyes strayed for a moment then she said,

"My husband calls, he and Tynan are fighting the gods, something they both enjoy much more than I. Their Dark side calls to it while my Light side shies from it."

"Yet you all must fight."

"Aye, Light, Dark, side by side for the first time since our prophecy was created, united by both prophecy and a common enemy."

Xali wanted to beg her to stay, to not leave her to her battle alone.

"I must stay with Sinow. Together, we are strongest."

"The reason you were called to stand among them. Never to have the peace you desire."

Her face grew sad for a moment then she gave a slight smile. "We will have it one day but not now." She looked to the northwest.

"Will I?" Xali braved.

The queen moved closer and crouched in front of Xali, the gold that rimmed her eyes sparkling with an other-worldness that took Xali's breath away. Her golden hair seemed like the rising sun, a glorious haze of silver shimmering upon it. She touched Xali's cheek, a warmth spreading through her mixed with magic that tingled as it touched each cell within her.

"I cannot promise that, but I can promise that as the Mother Fate guided me, I will be there, guiding you when you need me the most. You may not see me, but you will know I am there. You will not traverse this path alone, Xaliandri. But you must traverse it without hesitation."

The queen drew back and faded, a silver trail of sparkles left in her wake, floating gently to the ground. In the distance, the battle could be heard again, the gentle scent of lilac lingering as a juxtaposition to the violence.

"So, what do you want to do with the body?" Thane asked, unaware that the queen had been there, the conversation continuing. "We'll do what you think is right."

Xali looked at her cousin's body, still crouched down next to it. She ran her hands through Ainia's silver hair then down to the small blue gem she had always worn around her neck. Unclasping it, she slipped it into a pocket then stood, the queen's words coming back to her.

"We bury her. Her soul is already lost." She called to the land, roots and stems climbing from the charred land to wrap around Ainia's body. Then she commanded the ground to open. The body was pulled slowly under as the land gently welcomed it, taking it lower until the dirt fell to cover even the longest strands of hair.

Xali turned and walked toward the horses.

"I have a rogue husband to deal with and a spoiled bunch of pissed off gods to silence. Prophecy calls, boys, let's not keep it waiting."

She could feel their stares, knowing they were contemplating her sudden change. Mounting her horse, she freed Narilen's horse, sending it back home to the safety of the enclave. Then she looked to Thane and Cody.

"Can't keep destiny waiting," Cody said with a shrug, slapping Thane on the back. Then he paused, sniffing the air and furrowing his brow. "Why do I have a feeling I missed something?"

Xali shrugged and guided her horse away.

"I'd know that lilac smell anywhere. Couldn't say hello to me while she was here?"

Xali laughed and spurred her horse to a trot, looking to the northwest where the sky was ablaze with the war of the Fates and gods and the blackened cursed land that held the man she would either save or forfeit her life to, possibly both.

Five

The wail echoed through the halls of the Elvin castle as Ren shifted in. He'd sensed it, the sever to his connection to the Elvin king as his life had fled. His mother had once told him how she'd experienced the death of each Elvin ruler, their lives were tied to hers somehow, a link to their Elvin heritage. And so, as Ren had been contemplating his next move while standing in Tenebron, the death had settled upon him. He'd shifted immediately, knowing Garnevia would have felt it as well, worrying for the children she carried, the heirs to a now empty throne.

He'd landed in the great hall, and as he took a step toward the gardens where the cry had echoed, Paige came running from the corridor to him.

"Ren! What's happened? I heard Garnevia all the way to our chamber."

Another wail came, and both their heads turned to the entrance of the gardens. Paige gripped his arm.

"No," she said.

He took her hand and squeezed it, his grief set aside to help Garnevia. When would the losses stop?

"Yes, he's gone," he replied, walking toward the gardens, taking her with him.

Ren, Thane's voice cut though his mind. *Narilen—*

I know, I felt it. How?

One of the beasts. He was wounded too gravely for Cody's magic, claimed before we could even be by his side. Xali killed her cousin in retribution.

That surprised Ren.

Tell Garnevia prayers will be made, a pyre burned.

Thank you, Thane. Watch Xali, make sure that action doesn't turn her.

Like the others?

No, like my uncle. The Dark thrives in punishing the guilty, death fueling it. You know this all too well. Make sure that Darkness abates.

And if it doesn't?

Then we may have more to worry about than just the dead.

He drew away from Thane, adding a new concern to his growing list. Spying Garnevia on the floor of the gardens, he and Paige went to her.

She looked up at them, her face tearstained before she cleared the tears from her cheeks.

"Garnevia, I'm sorry," Paige said.

She nodded, looking away. "He knew, just as I did. Knew this would be his death. He believed in her, in Xali and the potential she holds for our world." She glanced back down at her hands which lie upon her swelling belly. "Our children will know the bravery of their father. The legacy he left."

She lifted herself from the ground, brushing Ren's attempt to help her away, her expression stoic.

"It does no good to mourn when so many lives are being lost. He is gone, there is no bringing him back. He is one now with the wind, and I have no doubt I will feel him as I walk, always beside me in death as he was in life." Her eyes met Ren's, and he could read the question in them.

"He will be given a proper burial. They have assured me of this."

"Good," she replied with a small smile. "Then his spirit will remain happy."

"Is there anything we can do, Garnevia?" he asked, not knowing what else to do.

"No, nothing can bring back the dead. We must grieve them then move forward with our lives."

She walked quietly away and neither he nor Paige went after her. Nor did they say anything more to her, knowing she needed the space, the time to grieve in her own way, in private. The throne of the Elvin had been handed to her until her firstborn was old enough to rule. It was a responsibility he knew she would not take lightly. It was one she had not wanted but understood it was expected now that Narilen was gone.

When she'd left the gardens, he felt Paige's hand on his. He turned to see the shimmer of tears in her eyes.

"There are always casualties, Paige," he said to her, bringing his finger up to stay a tear that had escaped.

Sucking in her lip, she nodded, pushing the tears back and summoning that bravado he loved about her. She was no weepy damsel, having seen enough in her years to know when tears were only a hinderance.

"Will you be staying or returning to the battle?"

He was tempted to stay, to hold her in his arms through the night and take comfort in the feel of her against his body, but he did not have that luxury. There were still mortals out there who had not been moved to the castles, those who had wanted to stay and defend their lands, ones too old to make the journey or too frail. Xali's people in particular were vulnerable, only a few hundred having been moved, everyone thinking they were safe. They'd been wrong and they were suffering for his inaction and that of the others. Every death that befell them was as though he'd dealt the final blow.

He shook his head sadly, drawing her in close, filling his lungs with her strawberry scent, his mind with the memory of her touch before he kissed her. The tenderness of the kiss was one to tide them both over until he was given more time. Lifting his lips from hers, he moved a strand of her auburn hair back.

"Be safe," she said softly.

"I always am. Stay with Garnevia, she'll need you close."

"I'm not sure about that. She's pretty tough."

"On the surface, but the Elvin in her is too volatile not to break through that exterior. Elvin emotions are fierce and do not like to be kept at bay."

"I know that all too well," she said with a wink. "You don't have an Elvin blood husband without knowing how their moods shift and effect the air around them."

"That's the Dark blood, Paige," he replied.

"Eh, it's a bit of both. Go, fight your monsters and end this war before we lose more."

"I wish it were that easy, but it's not me that the end rests upon. It's Xali."

Rage rampaged through Carnick's body, begging for release. He'd felt Ainia's death, his connection to her severed as her life was taken. It wasn't remorse or sadness that bothered him, it was the loss of a warrior. With her death, he had one less fighter to wear down the immortal king and his lackies.

He roared, fire and lava spewing around his throne. Ash rained upon him, debris from the battle of his gods, his dwelling situated at the edge of what had once been the mountain range. Close to the gods, his masters, the violence of the constant battle above, feeding him, increasing the darkness with every strike.

Sartria landed before him, her creature screeching as she dismounted. It waited for her, its hideous snakelike head hissing at the flames. They were all hideous creatures, but they were strong, with impenetrable armor, and unbelievably fast. Able to pass hundreds of miles in little time, allowing his army to cover the span of the realms easily. As Sartria approached him, he lashed out, sending her to her knees.

"I told you not to engage her!" he roared.

"Ainia is dead," she hissed.

"An expense brought about because of your inability to follow orders."

"We were just going to taunt her—"

He grabbed her by the hair, yanking her head back and forcing her to look up at him.

"Xaliandri is mine. You were told to leave her be, and now we have lost a fighter."

"Carnick—"

He pushed her head back down, slamming his hand to the ground.

"You obey my orders!" He turned back toward the throne but she rose, her fingers moving along his back. Something about the move disturbed him, the touch of another woman. It should have brought pleasure, but it didn't. This time it wasn't the repulsion of what she'd become, but something else that stirred below at her touch. He would have to contemplate it when this was over. She was the only option left now, whether he liked it or not. He would need an heir. A strange thought.

"Carnick, let's overlook this misstep. She draws near. Let us celebrate." She came around to face him, her fingers tracing the contours of his stomach, the feeling stirring within him again.

Turning quickly, he grabbed her face, relishing in the pain reflected in her eyes.

"Don't you have a husband to satisfy, Sartria?"

"He is but a lowly second born," she said, freeing herself from his grip. "You and I are first borns. Imagine what we could do if we ruled together."

He smacked her, and she fell hard to the ground. Anger flashed in her eyes. This time she fought back, venom in her words.

"Don't tell me you still love her," she spat. "That you wish to remain faithful to that bitch. Is that why you wait for her? Why you refuse me each time? To share your bed with her?"

He raised her with his power, gripping her neck, her toes barely touching the ground. "If you ever disobey my orders again, it will be your death." Her fingers scraped at her neck. "Xaliandri will be sacrificed to the gods, and their glory restored to this world through her blood."

"And who will share your bed, my king? There is only I," she rasped.

He tossed her to where the creature stood, then said, "No one. Go to your husband, satisfy yourself then get back to the fight. If you touch me again, I will take your hands."

She scrambled atop her viper, glaring at him.

"You will need a woman, a real woman when this is over. I am your only option now that Ainia is dead. You will come to me, and perhaps I will still want you."

He laughed. "If I wanted you, Sartria, I would have taken you. If I decide to take you in the future, you will have no choice but to satisfy me."

She flew off, leaving him to contemplate the strange reaction to her touch. Was a part of him still bound to Xali? He ran his hands through his hair and invited the anger in to quell the thought. That subtle feeling had been there each time, but this time it was stronger. Was it her proximity? She was close, Sartria had confirmed it, and he could feel that connection to her. She'd grown powerful, he could sense it as she'd struck Ainia. Something had changed in her, leaving her a formidable foe.

She's always been formidable, his mind whispered.

And now, she'd gone and killed one of his warriors. A loss he could not replace.

The ground stirred below his feet, lava bubbling across from him as the ground split open. He dropped to his knees, the god emerging from its depths. It shook the ground when it emerged, taking the shape of a man, something they'd been doing as their power returned.

"One warrior in this war is no loss," it said. "Rise, chosen one."

Carnick did as he was told, raising his eyes to look at the god. Its eyes were black voids, and no hair lined its head. Instead, a layer of armor covered the body from head to toe, the armor seeming to be a living part of its skin, black and thick like tar with ribbons of fire that flickered through it.

"You do not partake in the flesh that is offered you?" it asked.

"There is no time to partake in pleasure," he replied, knowing there had been more to it but not wanting the god to know.

It studied him as though knowing his thoughts. "She is a feral one, with spirit that will produce a good heir. If she survives. If not, my brother has his eye on her. He has a penchant for loose women."

Disgust passed through Carnick at the thought, wondering what was in store for his family when they met their end. The words led him to believe it wouldn't be a pleasant afterlife, and part of him wondered at the thought. Was it a blessing to know a god waited for your death to seek pleasure in your suffering? A nudge of doubt slipped in, and sensing it, the god stepped closer.

"You must focus on your goal. The sacrifice draws near and soon you will free us."

"Why her blood, my lord?" he asked, pushing the thoughts and the doubt away. "Could it not be another, so we are forced to wait no longer?"

"No, there is no other, all of you have been claimed. We must have the blood of the favored one to bring down the Fates and to escape this wretched prison. Your aunts were supposed to harbor our full return, but they botched it, spilling her blood outside of our prison."

So that was the key, he thought.

"It must be here?"

"Yes, and only here. A child of the Fates, of that wretched female Fate whose mates imprisoned us in the first place. Here is the only way. It is what your aunts were instructed."

"Where are my aunts?" he braved. He knew the one had died, having heard Xali's story of her death but he wondered at the other one, having not seen her. And what had become of the murdered one, did her body still lie somewhere above them?

"Punished for their ignorance. My brothers ate their flesh, and I drank their blood."

Carnick couldn't keep his stomach from turning. The way the words were spoken so nonchalantly, as if it were an ordinary thing, worried him momentarily.

"You fear we will do the same to you?"

"I do not fear anything, my lord."

"Good." It placed a heavy hand on Carnick's shoulder. "Your place is secure. Your destiny was sealed long ago. You will lead us to victory, to reclaim what is rightfully ours. Now keep that fool of a king busy while we wait for the sacrifice."

"Why is he not the sacrifice? He is a child of the Fates as well."

An intense fire lashed inside of him, the heat crumbling him to his knees.

"Do not dare question again or your secure position in our ranks will be removed."

"Yes, my lord," he managed with a whisper.

"Keep him occupied and out of my way. The sacrifice of your warrior led that cursed nature king to his death, but the Fates' child cannot be killed. He is protected by his parents and the others. No, he will fall when those damned Fates finally fall, and by my hand as she watches."

Carnick wondered to whom he referred. The queen? Or perhaps

the female Fate? There had been an acidic tone to his voice, one that spoke of betrayal and his need for vengeance. An ancient hatred that predated the queen.

"He can be captured," Carnick said as the flames dissipated within him.

"Go on."

"His wife has no power. We take her, and he will have no choice but to comply."

"No, she is immortal, but there is another who has no protection. The nature queen bears the heir to the Elvin throne. Find her. When you hold her life in your hands, he will be forced to protect her regardless of the price. See to it that he submits to you and he will no longer be a burden on your forces, his men will stand down, and the realms will be yours until we are freed."

He wanted to ask what would happen to him then, to have confirmation of his own position in the end, but refrained.

"You will find them in the Elvin lands. But be warned, he is a weapon of the Fates as his parents are. Just as you are our weapon."

"I can handle him."

"Can you? I sense a weakness."

The god appraised him, as if sensing that moment he'd turned Sartria down again, that feeling that had been there, subtle but still present. Or perhaps he had noticed the seed of doubt that had sprouted before Carnick had cut it down. The god lifted his hands, a dark force hitting Carnick, seeping into his being and doubling the power that he had already received. It coursed through him, turning him from his earlier moment of hesitation with Sartria, erasing all awareness of what he'd once been from him, and filling him with only hatred and anger. His eyes blazed with black storm clouds, flickers of flame outlining them.

"You are our weapon, never forget to whom you swore your allegiance, to whom you surrendered your soul, upon your first prayer to us. Take care of the Fates' sword. You are now on equal footing with him. Subdue him and bring the blood of Xaliandri to us."

He disappeared in a splash of lava, leaving Carnick to wonder why the king needed to be subdued before Xaliandri was killed and how they knew the Elvin queen was with child, something that he himself had not known.

Six

Thick black blood splattered Ren's face as his magic broke through the creature's armor-like skin. He sent one final blast of Dark power, shredding its internal organs, and it fell with a thunderous force that sent the land below quaking. Eoin landed next to him, looking as worn as he.

"They don't go down easily, do they?" Eoin said.

"No, they don't. It's like they're imbued with the power of the gods."

They had yet to figure a way to destroy the beasts without effort. They seemed impenetrable to every magic. Only when a weakness was found in their heavy hide could one be defeated. Each one howled with a call that sliced through the dark skies and carried over any distance.

Ren dropped his head, the screeches echoing through the black sky that showed no sign of the dawn that should have been, heavy black clouds eclipsing any light but the flickers of gold and silver seen in the distant remains of the mountains. The battle between the gods and the Fates raged still, a war that would only be won when Xali reached her destination. Ren knew this with an instinct that did not waver, one he'd inherited from his mother and one he trusted completely.

He didn't know how close she was to her destination, but he knew she had to be getting closer. Cody was calling him in enaigne at regular intervals to provide updates of their journey. Since Narilen's death, it had been uneventful, like Carnick had demanded she be left to complete her journey, awaiting her just as she'd said he would. Ren wondered at the impact of his cousin's death. Had it affected him or had the monster he'd become not cared about the loss?

Ren wished at moments that he had that cold disassociation to the death that surrounded him on a daily basis. The mortals who had remained in place, and there were many, were like prey sitting in waiting for their deaths. It was hard to watch, he and his Lightbearers healing those they could as his Darkbearers fought the attacks off. Each death sat heavy upon his soul, the Dark king in him calling for punishment for the injustice, a punishment that continued to go unfulfilled.

Then there was Narilen. He'd only known his distant cousin briefly, but there had been a bond there, one formed from kinship and friendship. His loss was devastating. Garnevia, as much as she'd put on the façade of the strong widow, still grieved, her cries penetrating the somber silence of the Elvin sanctuary at times, breaking the wall he had built around his heart, the Dark in him reeling at what it saw as weakness. Outwardly, Garnevia had taken on a determined resolve to lead the remains of their people, to continue in Narilen's stead until their children were born. His life would not be wasted, and his heir would take his seat when the time came. *If the time came,* Ren thought, looking away from the shadows of the Fates and gods in the distance to the shell that had once been his mother's land.

Cirillia, with its glorious fields and lush hills now lay in ruins, a charred, volcanic remnant of its former self, just as Tenebron now was. With every day that passed, the gods' poison sank deeper into the land, spreading further through the realms. Even if winning this war was an option, healing the land would take decades. He wondered at the Mother Fate's reaction to it, at his mother's. Knowing his mother, it was agonizing. The land was who she was, and to harm the land was to harm her.

Had the destruction of the land driven her? Fueling the fight in her. His gaze moved to the mountains again, the blaze of silver and gold among the shadow of ebony that hung upon it. Yes, knowing his mother, it had. He did not envy any god who stood in the way of that anger.

"Let us return home, get some rest before we head back out," Eoin said, breaking his thoughts.

"Wise idea, but we should head north, the beasts and their riders will not cease."

"No, they will not, but you cannot continue. It's been four days, visit your queen, my liege. Rinse the foulness from your skin and rest your weary bones, then we will return to the fray and let the others rest."

Ren nodded; Eoin was right. They'd been at it since the night Narilen was killed, and he was weary. A brief respite would be good, and seeing Paige would restore him as it always did. Sending his enaigne out to his men, he charged them to continue fighting, and those who had not taken time to rest, he instructed to do so. What was good for him was right for his men. It would do no good to exhaust them to their limit, for their magic would be weaker, their actions not as precise or consistent. He wiped the creature's remains from his face and shifted, landing in his room.

"Ren!" Paige exclaimed, running to him.

She'd been pacing in front of the fireplace, ringing her hands, her bright blue eyes dim with worry.

He drew her closer, tightening his grip on her small frame, taking strength from the feel of her, that hint of strawberries he loved upon her skin. She pulled back and looked at him, her fingers brushing along the growth upon his face, his face usually smooth or only slightly shadowed with growth.

"You look so tired," she said.

"I have grown weary of the fighting."

"And of the worrying?"

"Aye, every hour of every day."

"She'll make it, Ren. She's drawn closer, Cody and Thane tell you this."

"Aye, as of this morning, they'd reached the base of the mountain. But what happens when she reaches Carnick? If he kills her—"

"Shh," she said, placing her finger to his lips. "She will survive, whatever it is the prophecy needs from her, she will live. The Fates will not let her die. She carries a child, the heir to their throne, she cannot die."

She sounded certain, but under it, he sensed the forced confidence. They knew the Fates could be cruel, that happy endings were never guaranteed.

He took her hand and brought it to his lips, savoring the feel of it.

"Let's get you cleaned up then come to bed, you need rest."

He pulled her in again. "And I need you," he said, kissing her.

"And you'll have me once you've cleaned yourself. You reek of death and fire." She held her nose, waving her other hand in front of it. "And what is this black muck you wear?" She reached out and touched a spot of the beast's remains with trepidation, her face changing to one of disgust.

"You truly do not want to know."

"Is that? Ugh, that's disgusting, Ren. Bath, now." She put one hand on her hip and pointed the other toward the tub room.

Laughing, he raised his hands in surrender. "A bath it is, and then you shall warm my weary muscles."

She softened, and her smile lit the room and his heart, but then it faltered as the room shook violently. His eyes flew to the ceiling as small pieces loosened. Something pounded with a furry that rivaled that of the Fates themselves.

"They've found us," he said, his eyes meeting Paige's fear filled ones.

Eoin! he shouted in enaigne.

Eoin appeared within seconds, in the process of summoning a shirt. "Doesn't look like we'll get that bath or any rest after all."

"Take Paige and find Garnevia. They must be protected at all costs. Hide them somewhere, anywhere far from here and protect them."

"No! Ren, I'll stay with you. Don't send me away."

He took her hands. "You can't fight, Paige. These things are too strong even for us. You go with Garnevia. Keep her safe and comfortable. She will need you. Now go."

He pulled her close and kissed her, the taste of her tears now upon her lips, the lightness of the prior moment fleeing with them.

"Go, Eoin," he said, pushing her away.

Eoin disappeared with Paige, and Ren drew his power, shifting to the front of what remained of the Elvin castle, outside the sanctuary. They'd rebuilt it after awaking, but in the wake of Carnick's madness, it had fallen again.

The two Councils shifted in, flanking him, all but Eoin whose voice called frightfully to Ren in enaigne.

She's gone. Garnevia. She's been taken, her lady in waiting slaughtered.

Ren's heart raced as Carnick dropped down before them, the paws of the beast he rode breaking through the damaged marble below, the ground quivering. Ren walked forward, all three powers drawn. He could sense the change in his eyes, knowing they had turned a striking violet. He was angry, the Darkness demanding retribution.

Carnick leapt from the beast then drew himself up from his landing crouch. Ren could see the aura of power, a twisted Darkness that mimicked his own Dark power, the Elvin merged within, both encased by something more, that foreign power that could only have come from the gods. It shrouded him in a stormy mist that flickered red and black hues. His eyes were a violent storm of black thunderclouds outlined with a blood red that now lie in his pupils. Ren didn't know what to make of him or how to defeat the unknown power that lie within him.

"Well, well, you've brought me a welcoming committee," Carnick said. "How pleasant. Tell your men to stand down Fates' king."

"I will do no such thing, and you will not dare command me."

Behind Carnick more creatures landed, the rest of his family, all shrouded in that same power. Two were missing. Thane had relayed the killing of one at Xali's hands, so why were two missing? His eyes took them in quickly, discovering Xali's brother nowhere among the faces. Had he been tasked with stealing Garnevia away? If he hurt her, Ren would not hesitate to kill him, regardless of his relation to Xali.

"So, it ends here," Ren said.

"No, it begins here. You will have your men stand down and come with me or the Elvin queen dies."

Ren laughed. "How dare you threaten me." He took a step closer, the Darkness in him clawing for release. "You and your gods are a scourge on this land that will be cleansed."

"No, this land belongs to my gods, and you and your Fates have stolen it for far too long." He was cocky and far too confident. Why? "You know, when Xaliandri first woke you, I believed that the great king had wrongly claimed this land, that he'd stolen it from you and your family. But now I see that was all a lie, he was taking it back, reclaiming it for the gods. They will walk this land once more and soon. When I spill Xaliandri's blood, it will be over, and your war will be lost, everything you and your Fates have will be gone as a new era begins."

Ren ignored the chill that tingled along his spine at the realization that Xali was the key, just as he'd thought, the one who would turn the tide.

"And where will you stand when all is done? You have no land left. Your gods are seeing to that. The people will be slaughtered, so you will have no one to rule, and your queen will be dead."

Ren noted the slight still of the clouds in Carnick's eyes, the subtle shift of black to gray. So Xali was right; there was a part of the man he once was fighting still. Was it enough? As the clouds darkened once again, he thought perhaps it wouldn't be. Whatever the gods had done to him had morphed him into, the man below was lost.

"I will rule this land alongside them. Now enough talk. You will be my prisoner willingly, or there will be no heir for your precious Elvin."

Ren's heart stopped. He knew.

"My beasts will rip the babe from her womb while she lives and eat it as she watches. Then she will die along with the royal line."

He'd said babe. He didn't know she carried two children, but he knew she was with child. It didn't make a difference, if one died, the other would with it. If Garnevia's life was forfeit, theirs would be as well.

Ren, don't listen to him, his Darkbearer, Corsent said in enaigne. *It is only a trick.*

He has her, Corsent. It is no trick.

"What do you intend to do, mongrel king? Do you let my beasts feast this day or will you spare their lives, well, at least until I bleed Xali out as my gods are freed. Then the Elvin bitch and you will be theirs to deal with."

Ren, don't.

He tuned Corsent out and the others as they all stated their discontent with the ultimatum. Was this where the path had led him? A witness to Xali's death? Weak to fight against the plague that had descended upon their world? His Dark side balked at the thought. Weakness was not an option.

But was it weakness? If Xali turned the tide, if that was truly her destiny, then Ren's sacrifice would save the Elvin line. His decision rested upon his faith in Xali and a prophecy he didn't understand, nor truly know.

He dropped his power. "You will leave the enclave, your family removed from this dwelling," he ordered.

Carnick raised his brow. "You would command me?"

"Just as you would command me."

Carnick looked to his right and nodded to his cousin. She mounted her beast, the rest of his family doing the same. Ren commanded the Councils to stand down, silencing their rebuttals then stepping forward.

"You will not harm Garnevia or her child?"

"You have my word," Carnick said with a sneer.

"I'm not certain how good your word is but know this, if any harm comes to them, I will kill you, regardless of the power your gods feed you."

The ground rolled beneath Ren, and he teetered until vicious thornlike vines wrapped around him, securing him, their thorns piercing his skin, his cells healing the wounds to no relief as the thorns dug over and over.

"I would cease your healing if you want to avoid more pain."

Behind Ren, the Councils had tensed, but he'd commanded them to stay, and no one broke rank. The vines lifted, throwing him onto one of the beasts, the thorns tearing deeper, but he stifled the urge to grunt in pain, hearing his father's words, words that had been engrained in him since childhood: *Dark kings do not show pain, ever. Nor do they fear, fear and pain are weakness.*

He repeated those words like a mantra, the thought of his father giving him strength as the creature rose, leaving the Elvin Enclave and all he loved behind.

Seven

The horse bucked and strained, its intention to turn direction. Xali loosened her restraint on the reins and sighed. "I do believe we'll be walking from this point," she said, jumping from the horse.

She looked toward the mountains, the battle above raging, the clouds filled with flickers of gold and red, blackness engulfing the remainder of the damaged mountain range. They were close to Carnick, she could feel him. His power coated the area like an oily cloak. It had grown more insidious the closer they had come, and she wondered if there was any hope now of bringing him back.

Resting her hand on her stomach, she felt the flutter inside, movement that had started the closer she'd come to her destiny. Was their child part of it? She couldn't suppress the chill that ran across her spine. That feeling that he indeed was, that there was a reason she'd become with child so soon in her life, so soon after her joining with Carnick.

"Come, we'd best keep moving," Thane said, helping her from the horse.

She was an adept rider, but there was weariness in her legs, soreness in her back from the long nights of riding.

He and Cody sent the horses off then came to stand beside her. There was no need for supplies as other travelers would have required. Their magic created all they would need.

"There is something foul in the air here," Thane said.

"My husband," she said, taking the first steps.

They walked in silence, neither of them questioning the direction she headed, both knowing something drove her. She fingered the sword hilt as a massive crack from the sky shook the ground. Something hit the ground ahead of them, the force pushing it far below the surface, sending dirt and dust out around them.

She felt Cody's and Thane's magic protect her from it, but she couldn't tear her eyes from what emerged from the crater. The same terror grabbed her that had frozen her when she and Ren had first seen the gods emerge. It rose from the crater, towering higher than she could fathom, then took several steps closer to her. Cody and Thane drew their power, but she couldn't move, couldn't breathe.

"Good Fates," Thane mumbled.

"No, that is no Fate. That is a god," Cody said.

"If we weren't being approached by that thing, I would hit you with this magic for being dense, Cody," he whispered. "I know it's a god. It's simply bigger than I had imagined."

"And more terrifying," Cody said, seemingly not bothered by the comment.

"Only to you and your Lightbearer blood."

"Stop it you two," she muttered, annoyed at their banter.

"Sorry, I joke when I'm nervous," Cody admitted.

"Much to everyone's annoyance," Thane replied. "That thing is staring you down, Xali."

It was evaluating her, then it began walking closer to them, its eyes never leaving hers. As it came upon them, it morphed to mortal form, and even then, its power could be felt. Cody and Thane were forced to the ground as the god remained in place. They were as puppets to its power, defenseless even with the abundance of magic they held. The god's black and red rimmed eyes stared at her, seeing into her soul, searing it. His skin had a thick leather-like quality to it like a coat of armor. Within it, small spurts of lava erupted. Xali couldn't take her eyes from him; it was like watching a walking piece of the land—if that land were on fire. He stopped moving, going no further from his spot, as though something kept him there, allowing him no greater reach from the mountain's edge.

"It won't be long, little lamb, and then your journey will end, and ours will begin again."

Suddenly, she found herself in front of him, a force having pulled her unwilling body to him without her even realizing. He was standing so close now that she could feel the foulness of his power as it seeped through every pore in her body, touching her, clawing at her.

"I know what it is you carry." He stepped closer as her breath stopped. "He will never know that two will be sacrificed."

Her heart clenched. "You need my child?"

"No, but the blood of an innocent will feed my brothers."

The bile filled her throat at the thought, her hand instinctively going to her stomach. He grabbed her face, his fingers burning into her flesh. She stifled the whimper, but the tears of pain rose against her will. Cody and Thane struggled to help her, but neither were a match to his power. She knew they remained where she'd left them, stuck kneeling on the ground.

"Why not just kill me yourself? Do it now and end this."

If he'd had eyebrows, she would have said they had furrowed. His eyes squinted as he contemplated her words.

"So willing to die? You hold another life now. Are you so willing to sacrifice him? I think your mate will let your blood flow, and no other will do the deed. It is the only fitting way to begin our reign."

A thunderous clash rocked the ground, and he let go of her, swiveling to where Xali's eyes now lie on the Dark king, Ren's father. A swirl of black surrounded him, silver and gold shimmering within it. She stared in awe at him.

"Our fight wasn't over, Fioch!" His voice billowed, the power causing her bones to shake.

The god roared, but the king grabbed him with his power, sending him deep within the remaining mountain, stone closing around him as his body disappeared.

"Cody, Thane, return to Paige. Find Eoin, he has her. Your job is done here." His black eyes met Xali's, and she saw the brief flicker, the ribbon of gold around them dimming as he said to her, "Ren is waiting with your fate, Xali."

Her breaths came short as she saw the sadness in those black eyes.

"Sinow, we can't leave her."

"You are of no use to her now and a liability to your king. She is in no danger until she reaches Carnick. There her fate awaits. All of our destinies await. It is a heavy burden to carry, Xaliandri, but it is yours to bear."

His eyes hardened, and he dissolved to a cloud of black, tendrils within ripping through the air as he returned to the fight.

The three of them stood in silence, staring at the space where he'd been, no one knowing what to say. She was at the base of the mountain, but she knew she had another day's journey to reach the place where Carnick awaited her. A journey she would be forced to tread alone. But the path had always been hers alone. There had been others on it with her at points, Carnick, Ren, but they had their own paths that merely intersected with hers.

Cody took her hand, and the cooling touch of his healing magic erased the marks of the god from her face. She squeezed his hand, knowing she would miss his company.

"You'll need food and water," Thane said, conjuring both, a cloth container forming as the water filled it. Cody removed his cloak and formed a bag with it, Thane placing the supplies in it. Then he created a cape to cover her, the royal blue barely discernable in the darkness.

She brought her fingers up, feeling its softness knowing it would be a reminder of them, a bit of company on this final leg of her journey. Thane's dark eyes held emotion she knew Darkbearers rarely showed. She placed her hand on his arm.

"Thank you, Thane. For everything."

He nodded, squeezing her hand as he pulled his arm away. Cody drew her in and hugged her tightly. She took what she could from the show of affection, holding onto his strength, his goodness, the Light he carried within.

"My sister faced many choices on her prophecy's path, daunting choices that left her facing death more than she should have."

"She promised she would be here with me," Xali said softly.

A light breeze brushed against her skin, picking up the loose strands of her hair and bringing a sense of calm to her, as well as a hint of lilac.

"And she is," he said with a wink. "Whatever choice you make, she will be with you until she no longer can."

She took the bag from him and slung it over her shoulder, her sword moving with the motion. She fingered it, knowing she would no longer need it, knowing it would be useless to her. Removing her sword belt, she handed the sword to Cody.

"What are you doing, Xali? You may need it."

"No, you heard him. I am in no danger until I reach Carnick. Then it will be useless to me. Give it to Garnevia with this," she took the amulet from her pocket and placed it in his other hand, "so that she can give them to her firstborn child, and she will know the strength her husband gave to me. I don't know that any of my family will survive this. She may be the only family left when this is over. Goodbye, Cody, goodbye, Thane. Thank you for being my friends and believing in me."

Taking a deep breath, she walked forward, not looking back, knowing if she did, she might not have the courage to continue.

Eight

Ren woke from a hazy fog, the memory of what he'd agreed to returning to him. His head pounded, and he remembered Carnick knocking him out. He went to reach toward his aching head, but the vines still bound him, their thorns digging deep into his skin. He shouldn't have had a headache, his immortality ensured he would heal instantly, but then he remembered the thorns with their incessant regrowth, remembered that he'd done something no one but his mother had ever done, he'd stopped his immortal cells, staying their power, leaving him vulnerable. It had been a risk, and he thanked the Fates Carnick hadn't realized that's what it had taken to stop the automatic healing his body had wanted to do against the action of the thorns.

Pulling himself to a sitting position, he looked around, ignoring the wicked thorns as they tore deeper into his flesh. He could have easily freed himself from them, but as his eyes found the body of Garnevia huddled on the ground, ragged chains that looked like they had been formed from the rock itself around her ankles and wrists, he knew he had to keep his word to Carnick. She met his eyes, the green in hers lighting. She was weak, and he could sense the impact on the children within her. Risking it, he sent a wave of healing magic to her, seeing the change in her immediately.

A force gripped his body, shoving the thorns in further. He gritted his teeth against the pain as blood flowed from his wounds. The magic had a source he couldn't place, not one of the Darkness he knew so well. This magic came from the gods, gods who had empowered Carnick, making him their weapon.

"Don't try that again," Carnick commanded, his voice angry.

He was sitting on a black throne that seemed the consistency of molten rock. Ren could see the movement as if lava moved below its surface. He looked around the makeshift throne room, columns of the same molten rock rising above them. Below him, the floor was an enormous mix of rock, volcanic ash, and fire that rose in spurts throughout the room. No roof enclosed them, but they weren't outside. Instead, they seemed to be in a cavern of sorts within what remained of the mountain. Ren could see the ruptured mountain above them, the Fates and gods at war.

He wondered if his parents were up there, if they knew what he'd done. Of course, they did, they were Fates now, part of it all. The pain continued as Carnick rose from his self-made throne and approached Ren, the thorns lengthening, his breath short and strained as he struggled to resist the urge to use his magic. Carnick stood over him, a female cousin moving beside him, her silver hair slipping over her coy eyes as her hands brushed Carnick's back seductively. Ren raised a brow, and Carnick shrugged her hand from him. She didn't seem to notice, instead stopping to look closer at Ren.

"So, this is the precious King Ren. He's quite scrumptious, cousin. If you won't let me play with you yet, can I play with him?"

Ren glared at her. "That's Drostiren to you, and you will keep your hands free from me, or I will remove them in a much bloodier way than your cousin just did," he growled through the pain.

"Ohhh, I like you. You're feisty." Her fingers played in his hair, his stomach revolting at her touch. He tried to pull away, but the thorns thrust deeper. He sent his power forth, risking the pain, and she drew back quickly as it seared her skin.

She hissed and slapped him, but it didn't stop his grin.

"I warned you," he said.

"Sartria, keep your hands to yourself," Carnick said. "I swear I will push you into the flames if you do not stop your incessant touching. Go check on our Elvin guest, make sure she's not too comfortable after his interference."

She stood and pressed her hand to Carnick's chest, turning her advances on him instead, but he grabbed it and twisted it hard enough that Ren felt the sprain.

"You don't learn, do you? Go tend to the queen then get your husband to fill your needs. I told you what would happen if you touched me again."

Her spine straightened, and Ren could see her aura shift at the slight.

"Yet you haven't killed me, cousin. You will need a mate once yours is dead. Do not push me too far away, or your reign will end with you."

She walked to where Garnevia sat huddled still, grabbing her arm roughly and dragging her from the corner where she had taken shelter.

"You said she'd go unharmed!" Ren yelled.

"I said she and her unborn child would live, I never said what condition she'd be in," Carnick snarled.

Ren drew his power, the vines burning away, the Darkness evacuating the thorns from his body as he heard Garnevia scream when Sartria kicked her.

"Enough!" Carnick commanded, power whipping out from him

to snatch his cousin and slam her hard against the uneven terrain.

She snarled at him and leapt to attack, but he snapped her neck midair, her life gone before her body hit the ground.

"Pity," Carnick said. "One less fertile breeder to keep the blood-line cleansed."

"There's always your sister," Ren said sharply, sickened by the casual loss of life and the breeding comment.

Carnick turned his power on Ren, but Ren resisted.

"We had a deal," Carnick said. "I just lost a servant to hold my end of it. Now drop your power as promised, or I'll kill her now."

Ren stared at him, hesitating momentarily but finding no deception in his words. Against the pull of his Dark magic, he harnessed his power, drawing it back as Carnick's grabbed him, squeezing his body like a vice, bones snapping then repairing instantly, his immortal cells active once again.

"Amazing how the immortal body heals, isn't it?"

Ren fought the pain, thousands of years training to ignore it, keeping any reaction at bay. Carnick released him.

"Now be a good boy and sit still."

The vines climbed back from the ashes where they'd died, the thorns piercing his skin once again. A faraway look crossed Carnick's eyes, a wicked smile forming.

"She approaches. The real fun is about to begin, and you get to watch as her blood frees the true gods of this world. My masters will rule once again."

Frees? It seemed an odd choice of words since they were currently fighting the Fates after emerging from below the mountain. But they hadn't ventured past the range, had they?

"Xali is the sacrifice…" But she had been sacrificed, her blood drawn, the gods freed. Unless. "They didn't do it right, did they?"

"No, her blood must run through the mountain to break the prison bonds completely," Carnick answered.

So that was why the gods wanted her here and why Carnick awaited her arrival.

"Why not bring her here yourself?" he asked.

"The lamb must come willingly to slaughter now."

His words were startling, and the coldness with which he said them would have sent terror through any whose blood didn't run thick with Darkness.

Carnick returned to his throne, blindly walking past the dead body of his cousin.

Ren, Cody's voice called. *Tell me you're not on that mountain.*

I'm not on it, I'm somewhere in it. You're close?

Xali is, your father sent us away.

Ren tried to hide his surprise. *Why would he do that?*

They want her there, whatever purpose she serves awaits her wherever you are.

Not knowing what to say, Ren remained silent.

We're with Paige, she's safe.

Relief washed over him momentarily until the weight of the current situation set back upon his chest.

Thank the Fates. Stay with her. I have a feeling the end of this war is near. Tell her I love her.

Tell her yourself when you see her. Stay safe, nephew.

The rock shifted to his left, a massive catlike beast emerging from a slumber that had shielded it from Ren's awareness. It loped over to Carnick, chunks of molten rock falling from it with each step.

"Find her. Watch her but do not touch her. I want her guarded every step of the way until she reaches me."

The beast purred, rubbing its rough head against Carnick's outstretched hand. Ren watched as Carnick's skin ripped from the abrasive texture then healed instantly. It then leapt away, pouncing its way up the ridge of the cavern until Ren could see it no more, off to guard Carnick's prey as she made her way to his lair, to her death.

Staring at Carnick's throne he couldn't help but wonder why the Fates needed Xali here. Why not stop her from going? Why had his father sent her forward, sending Cody and Thane away? What was it she was meant to do that even his parents would lead her to her death?

The wind battered Xali, bits of rock and debris raining down on her the further she moved up what remained of the mountain. The battle continued above as if her journey were not playing out below. She remembered how majestic these mountains had always seemed to her. Dark and foreboding but grand, spanning the entire far northwest corner of Old Tenebron.

Now they held nothing but chaos and death, their beauty decimated so that their peaks no longer existed. Instead, they'd been demolished to piles of rubble and molten ruins, still high above the ground but less than they'd once been.

She curled into a crevice, wiping bits of ash from her face. Fear gripped her as she looked out into the darkness. The beast that had been following her settled somewhere outside the crevice. She heard the rock shift with its weight. It had been shadowing her for several hours, since she'd first begun her ascent, leaving Cody and Thane to watch her until even they were forced to leave. At first, its presence had startled her. She'd frozen in place, waiting for it to attack, but it hadn't. Instead, it had sat, watching her, awaiting her next move. Once her nerves had settled, she'd shrugged and continued her climb, noticing how it followed her, leaping ahead a little at times, other times lingering behind. It never left her completely, though, always keeping her in its sight. A present from Carnick she was certain, ensuring she didn't change her mind or fall to her death.

As fear inducing as it was, there was comfort in its presence, company in the encompassing loneliness that blanketed her with each step. She looked into the night sky, trying to discern its shape from the rock that lie on her every side but with no luck. Sighing, she tucked herself back into her spot and tried to get as comfortable as she could, pulling her cape tight around her. She thought of Thane and Cody, the warm fabric a reminder of them, bringing on a melancholy again, one that was followed by an anxious fear lined with doubt.

What was she doing? There was no turning back now, but her nerves pleaded for her to do so. It had to be madness that kept her moving forward, each step bringing her closer to her death. Would Carnick be gentle? She was inclined to think not, his actions over the past moons, the vile loathing in his tone when he had spoken to her, assuring her that her death would be anything but easy. An instinctive need to run overcame her, a motherly protection for the innocent child who would die with her, begging her to turn back.

She drew her knees up. Why? Why bring her unborn child into this? Why thrust his fate into her hands when so much already rested upon her? It was rare for her family to bear a child so early; her mother had been almost seventy years when she'd had Mendol. And there had never been one born before the throne was taken.

But then, she'd taken the throne, been crowned. The first of any of her cousins to rule, even though she was the last to be born. The first second born to rule in the history of their line. The youngest ever crowned, the youngest to carry a child. Placing her hand on her stomach, feeling how the child had grown in the time it had taken them to reach their destination, she cried. The tears flowed for the loss of all she'd held dear, the loss of her innocence, of her family, of Carnick. She cried for the child who would never know the feel of her arms around him, the father who would have loved him as she already did, cried for the sacrifice she was being forced to make. She cried until she could cry no more and exhaustion took her.

Her dreams were violent and disjointed, her sleep restless until a gentle breeze slipped over her, the smell of lilac, the calm she recognized, stirring her from her sleep.

Wake, Xali, the queen's voice danced through her mind.

Blinking away the fogginess, she forced her eyes open. She breathed in the lilac smell, letting it strengthen her, refresh her resolve. A silver light flickered in the distance, coming closer until she could make out the shape of a delicate butterfly. It flittered playfully to her, resting upon her outstretched finger. Its wings flapped gently against her skin, and she knew it was a sign from the queen. She'd promised to be there with Xali, and she was. The butterfly flitted from her finger, fading to a shimmering shower of silver that settled upon her skin.

The eyes of the beast appeared within the silver, and she pushed back against the rock. Its eyes followed the flecks of color, its paw swiping at it playfully, nearly slicing Xali's chest it was so close. Her heart was pounding, her breathing ragged until it turned and padded away, returning to its resting place.

Calming herself, she drew a deep breath. She knew what she had to do, the queen's touch a sign that there would be no rest for her this eve. She would climb through the rise of the remaining moon and possibly even into morn. The end was here, and she would face it, regardless of the outcome.

Climbing from her spot, she looked up to the sky, the stars just starting to gleam, the moon slowly rising to its spot in the sky, its partner no more than particles that floated where it should have been. She glanced to the beast which had uncurled itself and was watching her intently.

"Ready?" she asked it, getting no answer. Not that she had expected one.

Then she began her ascent once more. Step by step, she journeyed toward Carnick, toward her destiny. Through the night hours and into the early morn, the sun never emerged, the storm above shielding it. As she drew closer, the battle above stopped, the gods and Fates awaiting the next move.

Finally, she reached the place where death and her beloved awaited. She dropped her pack, knowing sustenance was no longer needed, and walked past the massive beast that stood guard, her own beast stopping next to it, letting her finish the journey on her own. Carnick's father was astride the other beast, staring down at her with beady eyes, the storm clouds within now a churning black storm. She looked away from him and walked on, thanking the Fates he hadn't attacked. He dismounted and followed her as she entered a cavern of sorts, its ceiling higher than her neck could rise. Columns that spanned the height were thick with molten rock.

Ren's eyes met hers as she moved further in. He was secured with ugly black vines, blood seeping through holes in his skin, and she had to restrain herself from running to him. Why was he here and why was he bound? He was strong enough to match Carnick. Then she saw Garnevia, bound as well but in chains, soot and dirt marring her beautiful features, her gold hair dirty and tangled. Ren was sacrificing himself to keep her alive, protecting the heir to the Elvin throne. That's why the king had said Ren's fate was waiting with hers. The last steps in this path were theirs to tread together, although they would be hers to own, he only a bystander to the turning of the tide.

There was so much at stake, too much.

Her eyes fell upon Carnick. She hadn't seen him since that day he'd turned, and she was taken aback. If not for the madness in his eyes, she would have thought him darkly beautiful. He was a terrifying presence, the power swirling around him, his eyes black storm clouds where flames licked the ridges. His beautiful silver hair was now striped with black.

"Xaliandri," he said, her name dripping from his tongue with vile contempt.

Upon his first step from his molten throne, the ground split open to her left, a great divide of spewing flames. Her grave.

She took a deep breath, the heat of the place burning her lungs until that gentle calming feel washed through her.

"I'm here, Carnick. Whatever it is you plan to do to me, I'm here." She moved closer to him, searching for any sign of the man she loved but finding none. Where was the man who'd held her close? Who had made her feel worth something? The man who had loved her unconditionally?

Her heart ached as she searched for him.

"Don't bother, Xaliandri. That man is long gone, dead and buried."

"No, he's still in there. I know it, somewhere deep down, he's there, fighting to be heard."

He smacked her unexpectedly, and she was thrown to the ground.

"Let her be, Carnick!" Ren called, and Xali could feel his power flare.

"You mind your place!" Carnick commanded. Garnevia screamed as Carnick's father grabbed her. "Or she will not live!"

Ren dropped his power.

Somehow, she knew Ren would hear her, and so she called in her head, *It's all right, Ren. This is my burden to bear.*

As she repeated the words his father had said to her, they reinforced her.

Carnick grabbed her arm, dragging her closer to the crevice, but she was quick, her years of training with him coming back to her, and she freed herself, toppling him in the process. Before he could rise, she pinned him, saying. "I still love you, Carnick, the man I know you are inside. The man who promised to be at my side always."

He roared, his power flaring, burning her, but she didn't let go.

He flipped her and gripped her arms so hard the bone snapped. She cried out in pain.

"That man is gone!"

"No, he's inside. You're there, Carnick. I know it. Protect me, save me and our child."

Something shifted in his eyes, the red receding, a flash of violet taking its place for just a moment, but it was enough to cause him hesitation.

She took the advantage.

"I'm with child, Carnick. Don't slaughter your own son."

The violet flickered again, and he pushed her away, stumbling from her, holding his head.

"Kill her!" his father screamed.

Carnick snapped his head back to Xali, the violet fading.

"Carnick, please, I know you would never do this, never hurt me."

"You thought wrong." He rose and made to take her arm again, but she was fast and positioned herself so that she pressed against him, his hand now pressed against the swell of her abdomen, and in that moment, the child kicked, as if feeling his father's presence. Carnick pushed her away again, stumbling back, holding his head. She could see the fight in him, the man she loved clawing to the surface, trying to free himself of the cursed power that had corrupted him.

"If you are too weak, I'll do it myself!" his father yelled, running toward Xali, his power drawn.

Carnick's hand shot out, killing him instantly. Time stood still as she watched his body collapse. Carnick roared, a sound filled with pain and anguish as the man within fought for survival.

"Run, Xali," he whispered, backing away.

She scrambled to her feet and Ren's hands gripped her. He'd freed himself and Garnevia in Carnick's moment of weakness. The cavern shook, the columns smashing to the ground.

"Come, Xali, now while you can."

She pulled free from Ren. "No, I can't. This is my path, Ren."

And that's when she saw it, the true reason for her existence, to satisfy the Fates, repayment for all her family had done. Carnick's eyes met hers, the violet fading, the man she loved losing the fight. It would never end until she was dead, and then he would be lost completely. Her death was required by his hand.

"Always by your hand," she said. "But what if it's not by your hand?"

A peace settled over her as she pulled further from Ren, finally understanding her purpose. She would leave them all, she would free Carnick, seal her part in the prophecy.

"Xali!" Ren yelled as she ran, her eyes glancing to him remorsefully before she turned them back to Carnick's, locking onto them. Her heart filled as the violet overtook the red again, and she jumped.

"I love you. I always have," she said, the flames rising to meet her, licking her skin.

"No!" Carnick screamed, running toward her, but the flames grabbed her, scorching her, the pain unbearable, the anguish filling his eyes until she could see them no more.

As the heat enveloped her, a coolness washed over her, a tingle, and a presence she knew. Her heart at peace, she closed her eyes, letting darkness take her.

Nine

Carnick dropped to his knees, staring at the place Xali had been, watching as the world collapsed around him. He'd been buried in a darkness that had consumed him, the talons of the gods warping his being. Their power had fed a part of him he'd never recognized but had always known was there.

Now he was back, Xali had pulled him from under the curtains of darkness, but she was gone. Her life slipping through his hands as he'd struggled to surface.

He couldn't move, couldn't take his eyes from the flames that had stolen her, couldn't make himself believe that she was truly gone, and with her their unborn child. He remembered hearing her words through the mist, how they had woken him. A child, their child. Sacrificed along with his mother. Sacrificed.

A howling wind tore through the cavern followed by a roar that bellowed, breaking the ground beneath them. The flames turned black as the gods were pulled below to the prison where they'd been housed before the world had turned to chaos. Debris pounded Carnick, yet he couldn't move, part of him hoping Xali would emerge, even as the world rained down upon him.

"Carnick!" Ren called, grabbing him and pulling him up.

He fought, trying to return to his view.

"Carnick! We need to go now!"

"No! I won't leave her!"

He punched Ren and ran to the edge, struggling against the overwhelming power that was cascading down and pulling the gods back to their prison. He pushed against it, fighting to join her, to leap in and save the unsavable. Ren grabbed him again and turned him, his deep blue eyes layered with sadness.

"She's gone, Carnick. She died to save you, to save all of us," he yelled over the noise. "Do not let her death be in vain."

Carnick looked past Ren and saw Garnevia disappearing with a Lightbearer. The body of Sartria was being shrouded in debris as the towering columns collapsed around them. His father's body lay sprawled upon the ground, flames slowly burning away any recognition of the man he had once loved. He'd killed them, along with so many others. Lost in a madness he'd been unable to escape.

His eyes fell to the black throne he'd sat upon, claiming his destiny, one that didn't belong, one that shouldn't have been.

The weight of it all came pounding into him, and he let out a pained scream that joined the angry roars of the gods. The throne exploded into tiny shards that scattered throughout his throne room, his power unleashing in his despair. The ground below shook, throwing him and Ren back. Waves of pain racked his body as the gods tried stripping the cursed power from him as they sank into the rift.

As the last curl of ebony mist descended, the ground rumbled, a screech of sorts that pierced his eardrum. He stared at the split ground, watching as a golden light fell upon it, awash with silver, the divide closing until finally, with an echoing thump, it was sealed. Closing the gods away for eternity, shutting Xali from him forever.

He crawled quickly to the space, his hands digging, nails splitting, shards of molten rock tearing into his skin. He ignored it, digging to find her, to reach her once again and save her as she had saved him. Moisture layered his face as he dug until Ren grabbed him again.

"Carnick, she's gone! You can't bring her back!"

He pulled Carnick up, all the while Carnick struggling to free himself, to continue his futile attempts to reach her.

"She's gone!" Ren yelled, shaking him.

"No, no. She's there. I can save her. I can find her." He heard the desperation, the lie in his voice as his body gave out. "She's there," he whispered as the despair gripped him completely, and he collapsed into Ren's arms.

Ren held him tight as the world caved in around them. Both mourning what neither could undo.

As the morning sun touched full upon the horizon, the storm clouds lifted. The land was healing as the Mother Fate and his mother blessed it once again, but Ren could not rejoice in the renewal of it, nor the feel of his mother on the breeze. Instead, he had gone to the southern castle, the first home of his parents, sitting in the shell of what had once been his mother's library. Now, it held only remnants of the beauty it once held, the calm it had lent him when he'd sat with her as a child.

He rested his head in his hands, having found a spot on which to sit near the remains of the dilapidated wall. What had it all been for? The cost of following the Fates was too high, their demands too taxing on the souls of their followers. And for what? To fight a war they had no business fighting? To act as weapons for the Fates, sacrifices for their entertainment?

The Darkness in him rose, feeding on the anger. He was angry, the ire stirred at the unnecessary loss of life on every side. Mortals, innocent people, lost, Carnick's family stripped down to a shell of what it had once been, Carnick now forever carrying the weight of loss and guilt that had come with losing Xali. Xali and her unborn child, both gone, sacrificed for something of which they should have been no part. The lamb led to slaughter by his Fates, the ones he claimed allegiance to, the ones his parents had followed through every trial they had faced.

Lifting his head, he stared into the shadows of the ruins, wondering how any of them would move on from this. How had his parents done it, time and time again? How had they had the strength because he certainly did not.

He sat there, lost in thought. Contemplating all that had happened until the air moved, and he looked to find Cody with Paige.

"Thank you, Cody," she said softly.

Cody shifted but not before Ren spotted the sadness in his eyes. He knew his uncle well enough to know he took things to heart. Under the humor and the smiles lay a sensitive man, a man who had grown close to Xali and was mourning her loss just as he was.

Paige came to him and sat down quietly on the stone wall. She leaned into him, and he brought his arm around her, taking comfort in the feel of her.

"You know, as often as your mother said the Fates had their reasons, I never liked that answer. I would never have told her of course. I think it was her way as well as your father's of justifying the things they'd gone through. Of softening the pain of it." She exhaled a long sigh. "There are no reasons I can think that warrant this."

He kissed her head, the softness of her hair sticking softly to the growth on his face. She turned to him, evaluating him. Her eyes held no pity, only understanding and worry. Her fingers traced the bloody stains on his clothes, his wounds long healed from Carnick's thorns, the imprint of them still held upon his clothing.

She brought her hand up to his face. "She knew what she was doing, Ren. Knew her destiny."

"But why was that her destiny? Why did *she* have to be the one sacrificed?"

"Is there another you would have sacrificed? Yourself? No matter who it was, the result would still be the same. Someone would be mourning the loss of one they loved."

"Why do the Fates insist on so much suffering? Xali was theirs. She was loyal to them even when she didn't know them. She trusted them—"

"Just as your parents did. Just as you and I do."

"Do you? I don't know that I do anymore. I don't think my father ever did to be honest. His faith was in Mother and hers lay in them."

"Then let your faith lie in me because mine lies in the Fates."

"After all you've witnessed?"

"After all of it. Trust them, Ren. We may not agree with the way they do things, but the outcome has always been worth it."

He wanted to note her optimism but didn't have the strength. He didn't see how anything could be worth the sacrifice that had been required. She brought her forehead to his, and he breathed in the scent of her, letting it fill the emptiness in him.

"I wish your parents were here, even Tynan," she said. "He would tell you to stop moping."

"And act like a Dark king," he finished.

"Yes."

"Is that what you want, Paige? For me to call the Darkness that stirs, that wants to rise against the emotion?"

"No, I want the man who is hurting to acknowledge that hurt then find the strength to move forward. Just as your mother always did without the Darkness your father held."

He moved his hand to her chin and lifted her face, those bright blue eyes heavy with the burden of being married to a man whose power either shielded his emotion or enhanced it, the magic within always at war.

"Come home. You need rest, and I need you." She stood, holding her hand out to him, but he didn't take it. Instead, he waited for a sign from his mother, anything to tell him it would be all right, a hint of breeze, a touch of lilac, something that spoke of her reassurance. He found none of it. "Ren," Paige said, and he met her eyes again.

Closing his, he called the Darkness forward, letting it overtake the emotion of the Elvin in him, the softness of the Light, letting it fill the spaces where doubt had sown their seed, where melancholy lie, before opening them once more.

He saw the brief sadness in her eyes, the knowledge of what he'd done to deal with the loss, then the resolve as she gestured to her hand again. She knew who he was, the parts of him that helped him survive, the good and the bad that came with having one of Dark blood as a mate.

He took her hand and stood, shifting with her, leaving his questions, his doubts, his pain behind with the memory of Xali's face as she had accepted her place in a prophecy that had required the ultimate sacrifice to bring it to a final close.

Ten

A warm breeze touched Carnick's skin as he stared at the green river, its playful ripples a contrast to his sullen mood. Spring had come early although he'd lost track of time while lost to the gods' power, so he wasn't entirely certain it was not on schedule.

The Fates had healed the land, the Mother Fate and Ren's mother bringing life back to the barren ruin the gods had brought to it. The mountain range had reformed and stood once again proud and prominent in the far northwest corner of Tenebron. Ren and his men had begun moving the people, resettling them, rebuilding the towns.

Weeks had passed, yet Carnick remained in the Elvin Enclave, far from the people he and Xali had been charged to rule, the reminders of her too strong in their land.

The remains of the family had been found, all awoken from

the cursed spell they'd been under when he'd claimed them for the gods. They'd suffered casualties, some to Ren, some to Carnick's temper, one to Xali's. All that remained were Mendol and Fairenth as well as their male cousins, Herind and Trevant.

Xali's mother had been lost, Ren killing her to save others. Even with all the protection the gods had given them, they'd remained vulnerable, all but Carnick to whom they'd granted immortality.

He stared at his hands, clenching and unclenching them. Immortality. Something that had never been his to consider. Immortality that still ran through his veins to this day. A curse he'd been stuck with along with the power they'd bestowed upon him. He would give it all up to have her here beside him again. What good was immortality without her? What good would it have done with her here? To watch her grow old and wither away as his cells stayed young and healthy. At least he would have had time with her, time to hold her, to touch her, to hold their child, a son he'd been told. The son lost to him just as she was lost to him. The son she'd sacrificed along with herself for him.

The endless well of melancholy threatened to drown him once again, but he didn't stop it, letting it unfurl its wings around him, blocking out the pleasantness of the outside world.

He heard footsteps and, hoping they would fade, ignored them until they stopped next to him. A shadow fell upon him, forcing him to look up. Garnevia moved to his side and sat upon the rock next to him, her hand to her swelling belly. He stared at her hand and sensing the pain it caused him, she moved it to rest upon her leg, pulling her dress to hide the swell. His eyes lingered, the tide of despair rising again.

"Narilen and I would sneak out in the high of night and come to this spot. There was no river that ran through it then, but something drew him here," she told him.

He remained silent as he had since he'd arrived, speaking to no one, lost in his misery, a tide that continued to sweep him under.

"It is said the river flows from the Mother Fate's tears. Tears she shed when the prophecy first sealed the fate of Violissa and Sinow. She knew the pain they would bear, the strife they would face, and the tears fell until the river ran for the entire span of their lives. Perhaps those tears were also for the others in the prophecy. Those we did not know about until now."

He stared at the water. In the past, he would have scoffed at the idea, but after all he'd seen, it was no stretch of the imagination, tears as the source of the river.

"There are reasons for everything the Fates do. Violissa knew this, Ren knows it, Xali came to know it. There are no mistakes, no missteps but those made by us. Xali was meant to die that day, Carnick."

"They sent her for slaughter," he said, finally breaking his silence.

"Would you rather she had died by your hand?"

"By the gods or the Fates, it makes no difference. She's still dead."

"It makes all the difference. Her death was the key to saving us all."

He stood, anger and pain unleashing.

"I lost her. No matter which way you and Ren twist it, she's gone. The Fates took her from me. I lost my wife that day. The love of my life," his voice cracked.

She reached for his hand as he went to leave.

"And I lost my husband. The love of mine." Her beautiful emerald eyes sparkled with the tears behind them.

He dropped his eyes.

"Their deaths were not in vain. Narilen knew he would not return to me, just as Xali knew. She gave her life so that you could reclaim yours. Do not let it be wasted."

"I have no life if she is not in it with me."

A tear slipped from her eyes as she squeezed his hand before he took it from her and walked away.

Walking through the Elvin castle, he ignored the stares, the whispers, those whose feet took a different path upon seeing him. He moved past the guards who granted him access to the sanctuary he had raided in what seemed a lifetime ago, kidnapping the same queen who had just tried to comfort him. He found his way to his quarters, closing out the world, letting the dark comfort him, thin streams of sunlight the only light. He'd been told Xali had stayed in this room, her scent clinging still to the space. He supposed they had placed him here to comfort him, but he took no comfort in the reminders of her presence. The clothes hanging in the wardrobe, the dress haphazardly left on the floor where she must have dropped it the day she'd left to find him.

No, there was no comfort here, only the pain of the past. He laid down upon the bed, staring at the tiny particles of dust that danced in the air, watching as they collided with each other, their paths crossing in no predestined path as Xali's had. He brought his hands to his face, pressing his eyes, fighting the depressive grip that wrung his heart until finally tired of the fight, he drifted to sleep.

His sleep was fitful, visions of Xali falling to her death, her last words echoing, the world crumbling around him as she and their unborn child were lost to him. The flames rose, claiming her, stealing her from him over and over until he was drowning in the flames themselves, the heat unbearable, the light blinding. He pushed past the flames, the light calling him.

Squinting, the flames left behind, he found himself in a field, the midday sun warm upon his skin, the blooms of wildflowers gently touching his fingertips. A breeze fluttered over his skin and there before him appeared the queen in a blaze of silver. As the silver faded, he saw her true form. Her golden hair shimmered with silver sparkles, her body seemed to shine with the light of the stars themselves, the emerald in her eyes almost too bright to look at, a golden circle around them, the same silver sparkles that graced her hair bouncing within them.

She was breathtaking, no longer a queen but one of the Fates themselves, her power cascading through the space. A touch of calm entered his body, her magic working its way in, attempting to assuage the pain, the guilt, the emptiness. He pushed it away.

"Don't," he said, knowing he risked her wrath.

She studied him, her eyes seeing far into his soul.

"You would carry all of it willingly?"

"Yes, it is my burden to bear. It reminds me of who I am, who I was."

"And who is that?"

"A murderer, a destroyer, a man who threw everything away and lost it all."

"That man is gone."

"No, that man is me. That part of me was always there, and it remains."

"Even the worst of sinners deserve redemption, Carnick."

"I killed my father, my cousin…I killed *her*," his voice broke, "and our child. They are gone because of me."

Her eyes grew sad, the emerald becoming a deep sage.

"She made her choice, Carnick. You didn't kill her. She was destined to die by either your hand or her own. She jumped so that it wouldn't be by your hand."

He looked down at his hands, seeing the blood that wasn't truly there, his mind never cleansing the stains.

"I murdered so many, gave the order to slaughter them—"

"At the will of the gods, gods who corrupted you. You, like Xali, now have a choice, Carnick."

His eyes met hers again.

"You can hide away in your grief, or you can take the next step on the path. There are players left, moves that have yet to be made, destinies that await."

"It's over."

"No, it has just begun. All is not lost, Carnick. I made a promise to Xali, and I kept that promise. Do not let the prophecy go unfulfilled."

"What are you saying?"

She gave a sad smile. "Things are not always as they seem. Look into your heart and listen to it. There is more to your destiny and my son's. Finish the path."

She faded, the bright world around him remaining. Listen, she had said. He had been listening, and all he'd found was pain and grief. He closed his eyes, pushing past the swelling tide of sadness, through the darkness, deep within himself until he sensed it, a connection. As if his heart were connected to another. Another that beat as strongly as his.

He woke, sitting quickly and saying the words he'd only prayed to say, "She's alive."

Eleven

Heat seared Xali's skin. It was unbearable, and she closed her eyes against the intensity. Pushing her body back tighter against the rough wall of her prison, she tried to steady her breathing.

She had welcomed death, remembered falling with a peaceful resignation as the flames and the weightlessness had taken her. She'd woken not knowing why, not understanding why eternal sleep had not claimed her. She remembered the cool tingle, the sensation that she wasn't alone, that the queen was with her as she'd promised but what she'd woken to was far from death. If this was death, she wanted to go back, this was a fate beyond death, a punishment for the sins of her forefathers, everlasting torment.

Pulling her legs in tighter, she tried shutting out the noise, the loud never-ending crackle of flame, the shift of rock far above, the screams that echoed, some with voices she recognized distinctly.

Her hands hugged her knees, pressing against her belly, bringing a wave of emotion with it. When she'd woken, she'd felt it. Her sacrifice had been of two, the child within her gone, wiped away with a fall that should have killed them both. No more did her belly swell or the flutter resound through her core. It was like the child had never existed.

She'd mourned the loss, countless time passing in a space that held no days. It seemed that moons had passed before she let the anguish fade, the emptiness within her subside. Moons for her to feel anything but hollow.

It still came in waves that would drown her for moments that seemed to last forever, a deep untethered agony for what had been lost. Then it would pass, the grief subsiding, leaving only the residual of hollowness, something missing that could never be returned.

She brought her head back up, staring out at the darkness, save for the fire that constantly roared, the flames like towering beasts beyond her prison. There was no light. She'd lost count of how long she'd been here, given up on her attempts to figure out where here even was. Food had appeared as did a liquid that looked of water but smelled of sulfur. At first, she ignored it, but then her resolve caved to her hunger. A part of her registered that she no longer needed food to survive, that her body simply craved the sustenance. A part of her now recognized what that touch had been as she'd fallen. The reason she still lived, the reason the flames scorched her skin, but the burns did not remain. Whatever path she'd been on had not been completed. There was more, she was still needed.

And she was now immortal.

Cursed by the Fates to live, to feel the desperation that clung to her like a sticky cobweb, at times smothering her so greatly that the need to escape this endless torment was unbearable.

But there would be no escape.

She lifted her head, hearing a faint sound that didn't fit the usual noises. A scurrying that led her curiosity to pull her from her corner. In the faint light, her cousin Ainia appeared, her face covered with dark splotches that could have been dirt or bruises, it was hard to tell. Xali rubbed her eyes, drawing back into the wall.

"Xali," her cousin called.

"You're dead, I killed you. Have you come to seek your revenge?"

"Hush," she said, moving closer to Xali.

Xali dropped her head in her arms, muttering, "No, no, this can't be." She felt Ainia's touch, the pressure of skin missing, but a touch none the less.

"Xali, it's me."

"So, I am dead?"

"No, only me and the others, the ones unlucky enough to have died."

Xali searched her eyes afraid to ask who else had died.

"All save your brother, Fairenth, Trevant, and Herind. All of us now bound to serve the gods and suffer their torment in every way imaginable." Ainia crossed her arms tight against her chest as if feeling their touch, and Xali didn't dare imagine what punishment she had suffered.

A mix of emotions battered her, relief that Mendol and the others, but especially Mendol, had survived, and a heavy sadness that her mother had been among the fallen. She pushed back the tears, not wanting to deal with the reality of the loss, saving it for another time. She'd already lost too much to bear.

Turning her focus back to Ainia, she whispered, "Ainia, I'm sorry."

"Don't be, Xali." She sighed. "Our souls were already lost, we chose our side, prayed our prayers, made our choices."

"Choices you never made on your own, ones our ancestors chose for you."

"And we never questioned as you did, Xali. We questioned our ways, our part, but never our allegiance to our gods. You didn't kill me, Xali. I was dead the moment they claimed me for their war."

"Why are you here, Ainia? Will you not be punished?"

"To warn you. The gods are not dead, they are angry that you cursed them back to their prison. I've heard grumbling. Their leader thinks you're something of the Fates', and he will destroy you because he detests them."

"Leader?"

"Yes, apparently they have one who rules the others. The Fates do as well."

This seemed strange, that beings so powerful would need or even want a leader.

"If they want to destroy me, why haven't they?"

"I don't know, but he is going to summon you. Don't test him, Xali. Don't do what you always do and question him. Obey and you may live longer."

"Live? Is this living, Ainia?"

"Trust me, it's better than the death that holds me."

She looked behind her, fear on her face when she turned back.

"He wants you. He's coming for you."

She faded, and something grabbed Xali's insides, stealing the air from her lungs. She was ripped from the cave that held her and pulled into the flames that scorched her skin. She screamed in pain as they burned her flesh, her body descending further and further. Burning then healing, over and over, the pain never ceasing until she emerged from the flame, a rough jagged floor breaking her fall and her bones.

She thrashed in agony as the bones repaired, the skin reformed, cuts healing. She couldn't move, too traumatized to will herself to. Her body rose against its will, her feet dragging along the floor. Lifting her eyes, she took in the god before her, the same she'd faced when she'd reached the mountains. He'd taken mortal form, his power-laden eyes belying his true form.

He dropped her, and she crashed to the ground.

"Rise, weapon of the Fates," he spat, then stared at her, the red of his eyes causing an uncontrollable shiver to course through her body.

"You would be wise to fear me," he said, and she bit back the retort she'd had in mind, Ainia's words returning to her.

She didn't know what to say, knowing anything she did say would likely bring more pain. Begrudgingly, she forced herself to her feet, the quaking in her knees threatening to send her to the ground once more.

"Walk with me," he commanded, not awaiting her answer.

She caught up with him, afraid to get too close.

"You confound me, Xaliandri. You brought yourself to slaughter, broke the hold we had on our weapon, then gave up your life for him. Resigned to die one way or another, all for a man who tried to murder you, whose every intent was to spill your blood."

"He's not that man."

The god stopped. "You think that part of him was foreign, something we possessed him with? You are naïve, child. That part of him was always there, waiting to be woken, tapped into."

"He's a good man, who would never have done those things without your influence."

"Perhaps. Or perhaps it was there waiting to be released. Waiting for its master to awaken."

Xali remembered the words of the Dark king, that Carnick favored the Dark. Darkness that could be tipped to terror.

"Do not turn a blind eye to what your heart refuses to see. Trust me, it will only hurt you more."

He began walking again, and she noticed they were no longer alone. Other gods were present, most in their overwhelming original form. The space they were in was massive, a palace of sorts made from the ground far below the mountains. She had no doubt that's where they were. It was glorious and frightening at the same time, a palace of smoke and fire. They were in what seemed to be a common room. They would have referred to it as the great room in her family's palaces. She wasn't certain what these beings would call it, but whatever it was, it was massive.

The gods stared at her as she walked by, raising their heads to meet her curious eyes. Two sat huddled playing a game, a makeshift board between them, creatures frozen with expressions of horror served as their pieces. In one corner, a god was mounted on a small woman whose cries of pain tore at Xali's heart. Her naked body tiny and vulnerable below him. As the god pulled her hair back, Xali recognized her other cousin Sartria. Her hand went to her mouth as Sartria cried, the beastlike god continuing to pleasure itself.

Xali turned away, unable to bear witness to what she lacked the power to stop.

"Do not pity her. Gaoth fancies her, it keeps her from the torture of the others. His pets do not get shared. It is a blessing to be favored by him." She shivered, wondering at the brutality that the gods saw as a blessing, thinking she didn't want to see what they thought of as punishment. "She would have stolen your lover, tried several times in fact, so do not pity her. She wanted to share the bed of a king, and now she shares one with a god." He let out a viscous laugh that echoed through the space, shattering Xali's ear drum. The sharp pain receded, and she could feel it healing.

"So, the Fates have chosen their warrior in you. You were meant to die, and so you did. You jumped to save your beloved, locking us away once more." He rolled his neck, the power pushing against her skin with every turn it made. There was something familiar about its touch yet something unfamiliar, like Dark power layered another unknown to this world.

They came to the end of the cavernous room, descending down a dark path, the walls closing in around her, the echo of the crackling flames behind them traveling with them. Finally, they emerged to a cave that reflected a lush green that sparkled in the rock lining the walls. Water lapped the rocks, the green reflected upon its tiny waves.

"Do you know why we are imprisoned here?" he asked, stopping before the water.

"No," she answered honestly.

"This world was once ours. Spite and jealousy stole it from us. Punished for daring to love."

That took her by surprise.

He laughed, a frightening sound that stirred the water, and bounced against the walls.

"Your Fates and my brothers and I were equals at one time. Glorious gods, powerful, beautiful, blessed by our creator. We roamed our world free of burdens, reveling in our powers. Playing among the same gods you now call Fates. We were all brethren back then, enjoying the spoils of our homeland.

"She was stunning. The one you call Mother Fate, Orlaina. A rare female in a world of mostly men. Guarded closely by her circle, coveted by Aodhan, loved by Diarmund, and myself."

"You loved her?"

A faraway look crossed his features, softening so that for just an instant she could see the god he'd once been.

"Yes, deeply, but she was never mine. Her heart belonged to Diarmund always. I could see that, but Diarmund's brother could not, his jealousy burned away the god he could have been, his Dark power destroying him, his greed for Orlaina eventually cursing us all. You see, I dared look upon her, angering him.

"When my brethren and I left, I dared ask her to come with us, to bless the new world we would create with her glory. She refused, her heart tied too strongly to Diarmund, her will bound too greatly to his brother Aodhan.

"We left, creating this world, reveling in the power of our creation. But Aodhan was vindictive, spiteful. Angered by my attempt, he turned Diarmund against me. Then he turned his other Dark brothers and eventually even the Light brothers who had befriended him. They caught us unawares, stole this world from us, imprisoning us here. Rebuilding what had been ours and turning it into their own world.

"Orlaina discovered us, as she was blessing the mountains but even she was turned by Aodhan's words. Their false world had been built; their people created by then. We were but a threat to remain buried. Her lover placed the final seal on our prison, she eventually burying us below the mountains, ignoring my pleas but not before I could curse them. You see I knew what she and Diarmund had done, created your kind, dared defy Aodhan, your race the result of that defiance. We hear everything here. And so, as she weaved her magic, I cursed your race, cursing their love with my final act, bringing Aodhan's wrath upon her and her children. Ensuring she and Diarmund would forever be left to long for one another as we were left longing for our freedom. Our race was cast aside and forgotten just as yours was. Your destiny tied to ours with my words. I bound your race to us, your fate to ours. Your blood would spill, and we would be free to revenge the wrongs and take back our world."

Xali didn't know what to say. She had so many questions that her tongue was frozen. She stared at the water, which had turned to a violent red as the story had progressed. With a lump in her throat, she asked, "Why me?"

"Your soul was ours, they all were, we made sure that in their spite for being cast away, your ancestors found new gods, our whispers carrying across the seas. You stood out in the infinite future of souls, inquisitive, proud, strong, and so we marked you."

"But not before she could," she said as it dawned on her.

He turned to her, his eyes now as red as the water, his shape changing to the monstrosity he was.

"She claimed you, somehow marking you as I did, seeing into my mind, my intentions, opening my curse to two paths. Then she claimed you the night you were born. I felt it, knew your birth was coming, the caverns shook with the expectation that they would soon free us, but then this space gleamed an emerald that matched Orlaina's eyes, her spirit within that light. I could feel her, as I once felt the touch of her fingers on my skin. She sealed your fate that night as much as I had the day I had marked you. Stole you from us, leading you to them through that child of their blasted prophecy, her voice swaying you to look away, to see past what the rest of your family could not. But your fate was still undecided still hanging in the balance, your blood still to be spilled."

"So, you used Carnick."

A cruel smile formed on his face as he shifted back to the form of a man. "Yes, they are our children. He especially, always diligent with his prayers, always turning toward our call without ever recognizing it. His soul as well as your family's have always been ours."

"He was but no longer. You have me, leave him be."

He grabbed her neck and squeezed, drawing a claw along it so that her blood splattered across him. She tried to scream but couldn't as he dropped her. Bringing her hands to her neck, she tried stopping the blood knowing this was her death, fear overtaking all thought.

"Calm yourself, girl," he commanded.

She wanted to scream at the absurdity, but she was too drawn to the feel of her skin repairing itself.

"You are not ours. You are theirs. Your blood spilt to seal us here once again at your hand, but it was Orlaina who ensured you remained theirs, that we would never own you."

The words were violent, the anger within each one like the slap of a hand to her face.

"What will you do now?" she asked, staring at her bloody hands, her fear warning her of the answer.

Pain grabbed her, excruciating pain that felt as if her insides were being split open. She bit back the scream until she could no longer hold it.

"You will suffer for daring to defy your destiny, you will suffer for her trickery, you will suffer for everything that you are to her and that damned child of the prophecy. Both their scents linger on you, touched by both and now cursed by both. And when we free ourselves from this prison, I will defile your body upon her bones until I finally rip that blasted immortality from your soul."

A force threw her into the water, holding her down, its temperature heating rapidly, water filling her lungs as she struggled. Her mind knew she wouldn't die but the burning in her lungs and the searing of her flesh told her otherwise. She let out a gurgled scream as darkness overcame her once again.

Twelve

Carnick raced from the room and through the corridor, nothing on his mind but Xali.

"Carnick," Mendol's voice cut through his determination, and he stopped, slowly turning to find him with Fairenth. He'd avoided them, knowing what he'd done to them, to all of his family. His sister's sad eyes broke his heart further. Did she know? That he'd taken their father's life? Guilt hammered him as they approached.

"You look terrible, Carnick, go get some sleep," Mendol said.

Carnick searched for any sign of anger, of hostility but found none, only sympathy. The hatred would have been better; sympathy was undeserved. He backed away, not ready for this conversation, wanting to find Xali.

"I know what you did, Carnick," Fairenth said softly. His breath caught, and he waited for her condemnation, but none came.

Instead, she moved to him and hugged him tightly. It was unde-served, but the warmth of it felt good.

"It's all right, I forgive you. My brother would never hurt any-one, especially his family. You didn't have any choice."

He pushed her away. "Yes, I did. I could have fought to keep my sanity, to stay by Xali's side, and none of this would have hap-pened. "

"There was no fighting it, Carnick," Mendol said. "We were all under its control, gods…Fates, I can still feel it in there."

"But I killed—"

"We all killed," he said.

"I was present when I killed Father," Carnick argued. "There is no one to blame but me."

"No, we heard what happened. You were protecting Xali. He would have killed her. Stop blaming yourself, Carnick."

He rubbed his hand over his face.

"Come, let's talk, you've sequestered yourself since…since Xali's death. We need you. I need you," Fairenth said.

"I can't, I need to leave. I think she's alive."

Their mouths fell open, and then Fairenth's expression changed to one of pity.

"She's gone, Carnick. Ren was there to witness it. There's no way she could have survived."

"I think she did. I think she's alive, trapped down there."

"That's madness. I miss my sister, too. Wish upon everything that I could see her again, but she's not coming back. She's dead, Carnick."

Carnick pulled away.

"You're wrong. She said things are not always as they seem."

"Who?"

"The queen. She came to me in a dream. I can still feel Xali here." He pounded on his chest. "She is alive, and I will bring her home. Mendol, I need you to stand in my place as king until I re-turn with her. The people will need you."

"Carnick, don't. This is foolishness."

He backed away then turned and continued his goal of finding a horse, hearing their protests but ignoring them. He ran past the guards, through the outside castle and out into the enclave, his eyes scanning for a horse. They were drawn to the woods, along the edge of the enclave, woods that followed the path out. The magnificent beast that had brought him and Xali that first night stood pawing the ground. He knew they weren't used for regular riding that they were special to the enclave, but the beast urged him forward, inviting him to ride as Carnick approached it. It knew, or perhaps it had been sent by the queen.

Either way, he mounted the beast then hung on for dear life as it took off at three times the speed of the fastest stallion. He knew then that he had been right; she was alive, and he would find her even if he had to travel to the depths of their world. He would find her.

"You need a break, Ren," Cody said as Ren stood overlooking the progress. In the weeks that had followed the end of the war, he'd thrown himself into rebuilding and relocating the people from the safeholds, never giving himself time to dwell on Xali's death, for if he did, images of her falling would flood his mind. Her face as she mouthed "I'm sorry" to him, the peaceful acceptance of a fate she'd never wanted. Inevitably, it would lead to his anger at what the Fates had done to her. She'd never had a choice, death always the outcome, just as his mother had never had a choice, the constant trials from the Fates.

Why was so much suffering required of those tied to the prophecy?

He ran his hand through his hair. Xali was lost to them and what he thought he'd seen in the words of the prophecy now confounded him. He'd seen her name and Carnick's far into it, not disappearing as she had that day. Was this the end of it? It couldn't have been, it seemed too short, too…easy despite the grave loss. The Fates never did easy.

"Perhaps you're right, Cody. I should check on Carnick."

"Afraid he might turn again?"

Ren shook his head. "I don't think he will. Whatever influence the gods had on him died with Xali."

Saying the words was difficult. He'd witnessed many deaths in his years, but this one had been the most painful.

"He wallows in the enclave, as though his life was forfeited as well," Cody said.

"In many ways, it was. Remorse is a wicked burden to bear, especially when combined with grief."

"Go, check on him, then spend some time with your wife. I'm sure she's tired of being couped up in the Dark keep."

Ren laughed. "So she is."

He'd left her there, the other castles not rebuilt, the enclave too close to Carnick, and although Ren was fairly certain he wouldn't turn again, he wanted Paige close to him. Besides, Paige was persistent and cheerful to a fault, something Carnick didn't need at this moment.

He nodded then shifted to the enclave, looking up at the Elvin castle that had seen its fair share of war. It had been rebuilt, the Elvin village intact once again. As was always the case, the calm he experienced in the enclave settled over him, reminding him of his mother.

He sent his senses out in search for Carnick, not finding him as he walked past the guards on into the sprawling opening. Puzzled, he continued, through the tree root that moved graciously for him and into the hidden section of the structure, knowing this was where they'd housed Carnick. He continued down to the room they'd given him, but no one was there. Pushing his senses further out into the enclave, he found no evidence of Carnick.

He brushed the weak aura of Xali's brother whose powers had

diminished severely once the gods had withdrawn. The others were the same, the few who remained, although surprisingly Carnick held a heightened power still. As well as the immortality they'd given him. A fact that Ren had yet to comprehend.

He followed Mendol's aura and shifted to it, finding him in the inside gardens. The girl jumped; he couldn't remember her name but knew she was Carnick's sister. The gray of her eyes was static, the loss of her power halting the storm clouds within. The sparkles of violet were barely discernible.

"You've come to find Carnick," Mendol stated, rising.

"Yes, but he is nowhere here. What's happened?"

"He left. Earlier today. Took off babbling about how Xali is alive, and he was going to free her."

"What? That's absurd. I saw her die."

"I know, we told him the same, but he kept rambling about something in a dream and how he had to go."

"A dream?"

"Yes," the girl said, "the queen came to him in a dream. That's what he said."

Ren's heart raced. His mother. If she'd truly come to Carnick, then there was a chance Xali could be alive.

Reaching out his senses, he swept through Tenebron, knowing Carnick would be heading to the mountains.

"Wait, you don't believe him, do you?"

"My mother only enters the Dream Realm when things are dire, or when it is necessary. If she pulled Carnick there, then I have no doubt he believes Xali is alive."

He shifted, landing far into Tenebron, surprised how far Carnick had ridden until he spied the Stiorme in the distance. The Stiorme were only found in the Elvin forests, and they were formidable beasts, their speed threefold that of a regular horse. The speed at which they traveled was stunning. Had Carnick stolen the Stiorme? He doubted it, they were obstinate beasts, never leaving the protection of the Elvin Enclave. More likely the beast had sensed

Carnick's need, urged no doubt by his mother's persuasion.

They were far ahead of Ren, and he knew there was no easy way to catch up. He aimed a distance before them, shifted and slammed his power into the ground, raising a wave that forced the Stiorme to buck, throwing Carnick to the ground. The beast spotted him and trotted to him as Ren smoothed the land and Carnick scrambled to his feet.

He made food appear, and the Stiorme nibbled from his hands. Carnick stormed over, rubbing his neck.

"Let me by, Ren."

"So, you can save Xali?"

Carnick seemed surprised that Ren knew.

"Yes, she's trapped in the mountain with them. I know it sounds mad, but she is."

Ren studied him then whispered in Elvin to the Stiorme, which nuzzled him before it turned and took off toward the enclave.

"What are you doing? I need him! There's no way I'll get there fast enough!"

"Calm yourself. Stiorme thrive in the enclave, he took you as far as was needed, now he needs to return home and rest."

"Then I'll walk. You can't stop me, Ren. I know she's there."

He pushed past Ren and continued walking toward the mountains, a determined look on his face and in his stance. Ren let him walk, then remembering how Xali had said Carnick had spoken in her head, Ren tried enaigne.

Carnick, I'm not going to stop you.

Carnick stopped walking, then turned back to Ren.

How? He looked bewildered at having heard Ren in his mind.

It would seem the gods granted you quite a few new abilities.

"I believe you, Carnick, but you need to tell me everything my mother said before we go to the mountain," he said aloud, walking toward him.

"We?"

"Yes, Xali and I are tied by that blasted prophecy, as much as you now are."

"You really believe me?"

"Yes. My mother doesn't enter the Dream Realm lightly."

"The Dream Realm?"

"The realm between the living and the dead, only a sparse few can access it and pull someone else there. My mother was one of them. Everything that happens in the Dream Realm is real."

"You mean she was really there? She pulled me into another realm?"

"Yes, now tell me what she said."

Ren listened as Carnick recounted the dream.

"All is not what it seems," he repeated.

"I can feel she's alive Ren, here." He pounded his chest as if by doing so she would appear.

"Then we will find her."

Relief overtook Carnick's features. Ren took his shoulder and shifted them to the base of the mountain range. It was an extensive length of land, running from the far northwestern corner of Tenebron almost to the edge of where the Sacred Groves lie. He looked over, seeing the groves that stood once again, replenished by his mother. He'd noticed the delicate touch of her magic, the scent of lilac that had swept over the land that day. It had sent the sting of melancholy through him, missing his mother's presence, remembering how the scent had lingered in the air wherever she'd been. He missed his parents, an emptiness had formed where they'd been in his life and his heart, an ache that wouldn't dissipate, muted only with the demands of the war, rising again with its culmination.

It was the same ache he knew Carnick had for Xali. There was no cure for Ren's heartache, but they now had the chance to heal Carnick's heart, and Ren would help, no matter what it took.

"Gods...I mean Fates, this range is huge. How do we find an entrance to a prison we're not even sure exists here?"

"They're here, somewhere. The battle was here, Xali and I saw them emerge. The prison is under us."

"You're right. They were trapped here. I remember him telling me that. They needed me to kill her on the mountain for the prison to fully release them."

"Him?" Ren wondered at the reference, the gods he'd seen were too monstrous to be given a gender.

"They take the form of men."

"Just as the Fates do," he mumbled, thinking on it. From what he knew of the Fates, they had created their people in their form. They rarely revealed their true appearance to their people, transforming to blend in or seem familiar, but they still held the shape of the people. It led him to wonder why the gods would do the same, unless at one time they had been like the Fates.

Were they connected somehow? Was there more to the past than what they'd gathered? From his experience, things were never as they seemed. The words echoed in his mind, similar words to the ones his mother had spoken to Carnick.

"Where do you suggest we start?" Carnick asked, interrupting his thoughts.

"We go back, regroup—"

"No, I'm not leaving here."

"You can't sleep here, Carnick."

"Yes, I can. I will comb this range every minute of every day and not leave until I have found her."

A drizzle began, and Ren raised his head to the sky, wondering if it had been his mother's doing. Sighing, he said, "Fine although I was looking forward to bathing this grime from my skin and seeing my wife whom I haven't seen in days."

As the words left his mouth it was too late to take them back.

Carnick walked past him, beginning his ascent.

"I haven't touched my wife in moons, I do believe you'll survive a few days."

Ren cringed, knowing he deserved the callous tone in Carnick's voice. He caught up with Carnick, deciding not to dwell on his inconsiderate words.

"You know I can shift us to the top."

"And miss an entry point?"

"If there even is an entry point." He grabbed Carnick's shoulder, stopping him. "Have you even thought this through? Say she is alive, beneath the mountain, held prisoner by the gods. How do you propose to beat those gods when the Fates couldn't? You can't just walk in there and take her."

Carnick's eyes grew stormy, the flickers of violet brighter.

"What if it were your wife?"

The thought terrified Ren, angering his Dark side, calling it to quell the feeling. He'd almost lost her once, thought he had, and the heartache had been the hardest thing he'd had to bear, as painful as the loss of his parents had been.

He nodded, squeezing Carnick's arm. "Let's go. We'll figure out a plan as we search or like everything else with Xali, we'll figure it out when we get there."

Carnick laughed. "I see you finally understand how she works."

"Anyone who thinks it would be interesting to wake an immortal Dark king and his unsteady brother after they've been asleep for ten thousand years is clearly not someone who thinks her actions through."

Carnick gave a hearty chuckle, and it was good to hear him do so. As they searched, they talked, learning each other's histories, their personalities, finding they were more similar than either had thought. A comradeship began to build, deeper than the surface one they'd had when Xali had first taken the throne, an unlikely friendship between two former adversaries.

They settled that night on a patch of flat rock, the rain having abated and a gentle snow beginning to fall. Both were exhausted, the terrain brutal and unforgiving, Both had fallen multiple times, their immortality ensuring their survival. Ren grumbled about not shifting through most of the climb, insisting they shift in places where they could not pass.

As he drew a fire with his magic, he looked at Carnick and frowned.

"We can't continue on foot, Carnick. I'll pull a few men, have them search the western and eastern corners while we continue to the center. This is too much for just the two of us. I let you have your way today, but tomorrow, we use our gifts. There's no sense in having our powers if we don't use them."

"I can't shift, Ren, and I won't have you dragging me around like some child."

Ren sat further from the fire, the Darkness providing its own internal heat.

"Why can't you shift?"

"I don't know. I don't have Xali's powers."

"No, but your powers derive from the same source, and now you have magic the gods gave you."

Carnick seemed taken aback. Ren had suspected Carnick thought they hadn't discovered that all of his power hadn't returned to the gods. The immortality was obvious, the rest not so much, but Ren could sense it.

"There's a distinct pattern to the magic they gave you while you were lost to them. It's foreign from the other three powers of our world."

Carnick squeezed his hands in and out, staring at the flames. "I didn't think anyone would notice. I'm not a threat, Ren. I won't ever turn back into that monster."

Ren studied him, sensing the magic in his aura, the Darkness that clung to it like the spark of flint. Was there certainty to his words? Any way to guarantee the power wouldn't meet that spark again and turn him? Darkness was a fickle power and given the right source, it overcame all else. But Carnick was a blend of magic, just as Ren was, three magics within one man. With Carnick, however, there was no counter to the three volatile powers. No Light to calm the Dark and Elvin that hungered for release, nor to calm the foreign power. Could it be calmed or was the nature gift in him the balance just as the Light was in Ren?

A breeze drifted across his skin, stirring the snowflakes that had grown larger.

"Lilac," Carnick mumbled.

Ren smiled at his mother's touch, her acknowledgment that his thought was true. The Elvin within Carnick acted differently than it did in Ren or even his mother. It wasn't the catalyst that brought the Darkness to the forefront but rather the balance between two very similar powers. Powers from formidable creators, ones that strove for dominance. As if the gods and Dark Fates were warring within him, the Mother Fate the barrier separating them, taking the good qualities of both and creating something new.

He thought about his parents. Their prophecy had healed a rivalry between two brother Fates over the Mother Fate, a rivalry which had left them as broken as the prophecy had left his parents, the journey his parents had taken, healing that rift. That was the story his mother had once told him. He was the result of all of it, a harmony between the three lines of powers, uniting the people and the Fates. They'd never quite understood the part of the Light within him, how it had been essential to the peace the prophecy had brought to that past the Fates held, but he suspected there was a story to it. There was a purpose to every piece of the prophecy and to everything the Fates did.

Was Carnick the same? An end result to some rift that had caused the gods to be imprisoned? Had the gods unknowingly made him so? He thought of the writing on the guardian's lair, Xali's name merged with his own, their paths intertwined but Carnick there as well. He hadn't focused on Carnick when he'd taken it in, thinking Xali was the main piece, the key, but perhaps she and Ren were simply instigators, the spark to whatever was meant to happen.

But what was the end result? The goal of all of this?

He ran his hand through his hair.

"Ren? You all right?"

Ren looked up, meeting Carnick's eyes as it dawned on him. It wasn't Carnick or Xali who was the outcome, it was their child. A true blend of the powers that were a force in this world. He put his hand down on the ground to steady himself as the snow danced around him. A child to an immortal. Would the child then be immortal, creating a new line?

"Ren, you look like the shades have risen from the pyres. What is wrong?"

"A son. Xali was carrying a son, but what if…what if that son was the sacrifice the Fates traded for Xali's life?"

Ren sensed the Darkness rise in Carnick.

"Our child? They sacrificed an unborn child—"

"To save Xali."

Carnick sat back, the shock overtaking the anger. "But why and how?"

"If Xali's blood was required, the child would have had her blood. She sacrificed both their lives to save us but only one was required, and Xali is still needed in all of this."

"That would imply the Fates knew all of this would happen, that they were cruel enough to kill an unborn child."

"For the sake of the one needed to bring the prophecy to fruition. You'd be surprised how cruel the Fates can be."

"Then our line ends. There will be no heir if the child is lost, our family eradicated."

"No," Ren said, shaking his head. "Too much has gone into this, the Mother Fate still has a vested interest in your line. She is your creator. She would never let her children die. You'll find the Fates to be cruel but very protective."

"Your mother said only one child shall be born from each generation."

"Born…this child was never born Carnick." He stood, pacing the small space, his shoes sinking in the layering snow. "If Xali is alive, your heir will still be born, this child was not meant to be, never part of your future."

"It was early," Carnick said slowly. "Our family never bears children until well into their reign, my mother was eighty when I was born. Xali is a mere eighteen years, I only twenty-eight. We should not have produced an heir so early."

"You weren't meant to, and you won't."

A thought crossed his mind, and he wondered at the immortality that Carnick had gained. What did it mean for Xali? Or was there a reason she'd survived her plummet to the gods' prison? Were they both now immortal? Would their future child be so? Two immortals to rule their world again, but why?

"A merging, one final merging of all the races. Fates, this is the Mother Fate's play at her own redemption for letting them turn her children away, for letting any of this happen." He turned to Carnick, stopping his pacing. "You are destined to have a female heir."

Carnick stared at him in disbelief, but Ren knew he was right, instinct nudging him, that trait he'd inherited from his mother, one that was less frequent than hers but strong when it appeared, telling him this was true.

"Dark kings, Light kings always bear a son, my mother's birth the only exception because the Elvin in her was strong."

"What are you saying, Ren?"

"That we are simply players in a very long game. My parents' fate led to my birth, a merging of the three powers. Our heirs are the final play in that prophecy, the merging of all the blood lines, perhaps a redemption for something more than the Mother Fate's children, for something even greater."

"For crimes against the gods," Carnick said quietly.

"Our children will make amends for the wrongs that were committed, whatever wrongs that might be. They will be the redemption. And heal the final rift this world bears."

His words hung in the air, a strange silence following, even the wind and snow halting. The Fates and the world had stopped to hear his words. His eyes drifted to the sky, and he wondered at the sheer power of the Mother Fate. To have weaved a prophecy this determined, this powerful. Some part of him wondered if even the other Fates had been blind to her final plan. Would there be consequences if they had been? And would those consequences change Xali's fate? As if in answer, a rumble of thunder could be heard in the distance.

His eyes met Carnick's, and a sense of urgency called to him. Having the same realization, Carnick said, "We'd better find her quickly. I don't know if her fate is as secure as it once was."

"Damn," Ren muttered, cursing himself for thinking out loud. If the other Fates turned on the Mother Fate, what did that mean for their future? For the future of Carnick's people? What did it mean for Ren's parents? Or was that yet another play by the Mother Fate, a manipulation to give her numbers if the Dark Fates did turn on her? There was safety in numbers and safety in having his parents and his uncle close.

The sky to the east grew dark, thick billowing clouds of black encompassing it. The thunder rumbled, followed by green and purple streaks of lightning. The wind whipped around them as a war began far above.

"No, I don't think it is," he said, the clouds spreading to cover even the mountains, the top of which were now indiscernible from them. Snow pelted them with a fury, the wind stirring it so that it assaulted everything in its path. He threw a shield around them and stepped closer to the mountainside as Carnick did the same. "I don't think any of our fates are as secure as they once were."

"Then you'd best start praying to your parents that they find a way to calm the moods of the other Fates, or all is lost."

Ren stared at the flashes of green and purple that were startling against the black clouds, occasional flickers of arcane blue accompanying them. Even the Light Fates had joined the fight. The purple he knew was his mothers, all of her powers called upon, something she rarely did. Dropping his eyes, he sent them a prayer, hoping they heard, hoping it was any use, praying his words hadn't been the catalyst to an unexpected doom.

Thirteen

The dark did little to abate the heat of her prison, but Xali didn't notice. Pain racked her body, continuous, torturous pain, the flames from below internally licking at her insides. Never ceasing. It was torture, and she knew it would never end. She was the sacrifice, the one who would suffer for the actions the gods saw as crimes, the Fates standing aside for her to take the punishment. The day she had cast herself into the world below, she'd taken their place.

The war had ended, but her battle had only begun.

"Why?" she cried in a whisper.

There would have been tears, but none remained. She'd cried as the pain had torn through her too many times. Instead, her body went through the movements as though she was sobbing, dry crying, each move causing more discomfort.

Ainia did not return, and Xali had lost track of how many days she'd been here. There were no windows to the outside world to view the cycles of the sun and moons. Moons…had they been repaired? Had the world that had been in a state of sheer devastation been returned to its previous state? Had Ren and his men seen to it that all was restored to how it had been before the war, before the turning of her family, of Carnick?

The thought of him caused another violent sob, dry and painful. Was he better? Had he returned to who he'd always been? The man she loved. In that moment that she'd jumped, she'd seen it, the shift in his eyes, the red lifting, the glimmer of violet resurfacing. She prayed to the Fates that he had remained that way.

She wrapped her arms tighter around her waist as another sob threatened to escape. She missed him, his touch, his face, his laughter. If she could only go back to the days before all of this had forever severed them from their youth, the innocence they'd had. Would she give up the immortals for that? Before the war, she would have said no, but now? She wasn't so certain. Their return had changed everything…but it hadn't been them, had it? It had been her aunts and their selfish need for power. Once again, her family putting their needs before the good of everyone. Cursed. Her family had been a curse on this world, an abomination that had changed it forever. And she was paying the price.

Movement drew her attention from her self-pity, and she lifted her eyes, ignoring the pain the action caused. Across from her sat Sartria, her hair knotted and stringy, her eyes swollen from crying, bruises lining her arms and legs. She wore a light linen dress that looked more fit for a child then a grown woman, its length barely reaching her mid-thigh, its thick straps falling to reveal the marred flesh below.

Sartria had always been the hardest on her, the one to tease her relentlessly until one day it had stopped, but the side-glances and snide remarks had not. Nor had the constant looks to Carnick, inappropriate comments, touches made certain to be seen by Xali.

Regardless, her punishment was extreme, and all Xali felt for her was pity.

Sartria lifted her eyes, the storm clouds no more, gone with the loss of her life and her power. All that remained was a dull, lifeless gray.

"I'm sorry, Xali," she said softly. "Sorry for all of it. I…I tried to take Carnick when we were…when we were under the gods' influence. I tried, just as I tried so many times in the past. I…" She turned her head away, tears spilling. "He killed me. Killed me when I wouldn't listen, wouldn't stop. Even then, he loved you, even lost to that horrible, corrupt magic. I never saw it before, never wanted to believe it. None of us loved each other like that, all of us duty bound to love. But you and Carnick…" She looked back at Xali, the remorse spilling over with her tears. Then, she rose and turned to leave.

Xali grabbed her hand, the movement slicing daggers through her body as every movement did. Sartria glanced back at her hand then met her eyes.

"You are still my cousin, Sartria. You were always hard on me, but you made me stronger for it. I knew you wanted Carnick to yourself, that you wanted what was mine—"

"I could never have had what was yours, Xaliandri. You were different than the rest of us. Brave, sure of yourself, even without magic, strong by your own means and not through that magic. I wanted what you had because I envied it."

Squeezing her hand, Sartria leaned down and brushed the hair back from Xali's face, bringing herself down to where Xali still lay on the floor. "Now I've lost everything and will never know what it's like to have what you have. You still have life, Xali." Her voice dropped to a whisper. "Find that strength again and escape this place."

"I can't. This is my destiny, my sacrifice."

"But you have already sacrificed so much, little cousin. We are lost, but you…you are still who you were when we were children.

Obstinate, stubborn, determined, filled with something none of us could understand." Her fingers pulled back, her eyes searching Xali's. "Whatever that was, find it again and free yourself."

"Not without you and Ainia."

"We are not the only ones, cousin. All of us are here in some form. Ainia and I slaves to them, the others I do not know where their souls are kept, but they are here. All of us, prisoners for eternity."

Xali let a sob escape, the thought of her mother and father here, the others who had fallen before and during the war, all of their souls owned by the ones to which they had sworn their allegiance.

"Hush, now little cousin. Find your way home to Carnick. Tell Herind that I'm sorry, for everything." She kissed Xali's head and rose, scurrying away before Xali could stop her. The flames outside her cell rose, the heat barely tolerable as a massive roar shook the cavern. Xali knew her cousin had snuck away, her captor unknowing until this moment. What wrath had she risked to do so? And why had it been so important to her to absolve her crimes, to encourage Xali to find her strength?

Xali stared at the space where she had been, mourning her cousin and the others in her family who had succumbed to the actions of themselves and those around them. Some to her, some to Carnick, others to fate. Sighing, she gave herself over to the incessant rhythm of pain and healing that had been her only constant in the lonely cell, praying to anyone who could hear that the end would come for she didn't know how much more she could bear before her sanity fled her side, joining everything else she had lost.

Carnick hunched against the rock, the wind battering the shields he and Ren had created, hail pounding it in an irritating clicking that was maddening. They'd been stuck as the Fates began their own battle, the world a chaotic blend of abusive weather and beautiful lights that decorated the sky above. It had been that way for what seemed like days. Ren had wanted to shift, but Carnick refused. He would not leave the mountain until Xali was in his arms, no matter what assaulted him in the process. Ren had stayed by his side, a constant companion, all the while Carnick knowing he wanted to be in Paige's arms. He'd tried sending Ren away, at least for a short respite from the storm, but Ren wouldn't have it. His choice had been made to follow Carnick through on this journey, no matter the consequence.

Ren created a small fire, sweet bread, and ale for them both. As he had each time, Carnick ignored the food and took the drink, hoping for some dulling of the senses but never finding it. He stared at the cup after a few large swigs.

"The magic of immortality burns away the effects of the alcohol. No matter how much you drink, it will not help you escape, or so my father once told me."

Carnick looked up at him. "No effect? So not only am I cursed with this never-ending life, but I can't even drink my way through it with pleasure?"

Ren chuckled. "I'm afraid not. You could drink a hundred cups of it and still have your wits about you."

He lowered his mug. "You are a boring lot, aren't you?"

"And now you are one of us. Welcome to the boring life." Ren glanced around at the storm beyond the shield. "Although I'd wager to say this is anything but boring."

Carnick followed his eyes. The dark clouds had moved in, shielding the sun and the moon so that their cycles could no longer be counted. He had no idea if it was night or day above those clouds.

"Do you think it will ever stop?" he asked.

Ren shrugged. "I've no idea. None of us has yet to figure the Fates out, and each time we do, we find we were wrong. They befuddle us constantly. "

"They're an unruly bunch, aren't they? I mean the way this

weather shifts, you'd think it were a woman's temperament."

"Ha! Don't ever let my wife hear you say that, or she will show you her temperament, and trust me, you don't want to be on the receiving end of that."

Carnick smiled, an act that seemed foreign to him.

"Tell me about Paige since we're stuck here. She's the one thing you haven't shared in this time you've been attached to my hip like a shadow."

The glare that came from Ren would have frightened any man but not Carnick. He winked and took a chug of the pointless ale.

"I am not attached to you like a shadow. I am accompanying you so you don't do something rash or foolish."

"Shadowing me. Now tell me about her. Why does it seem as if she's known your mother for forever and how did she come to be so welcome in your father's presence?"

"Paige is unique, and she has known my mother for what some might call forever. Long before I was born in fact."

That surprised Carnick, and Ren must have read the confusion on his face.

"That is a very long story," he said, running his fingers around the rim of his drink.

"Well, we have plenty of time. I don't think this storm or the family squabble above us is stopping any time soon."

"Aye, you're likely right about both of those facts. I will give you the abbreviated version. Paige was never meant to be immortal. She was born a mortal, and for all purposes, she was supposed to remain that way. But, as always, there is more to be seen with the Fates than we see on the surface or even when we step onto their path. She was integral in saving my mother and reuniting my parents long before I was born, before they were even married. Without her, the outcome may have been different.

"I had occasion to meet her briefly when my uncle played with time, bending it to his will and sending me back to my parents' youth. It was then that I met her and fell in love with her. You see, immortals in my line are called to our mates. There is only one and the call is strong. Paige is my mate. I knew it then as I left her in the past, expecting to never see her again, expecting that my line would end with me, for only a mate can bear the heir of an immortal."

"You lost her?" Carnick asked, still trying to wrap his head around the idea that time had been distorted and Ren taken to his parents' past. The impossibility of it was overwhelming, the sheer power it spoke of astounding.

"Yes, but when I returned to this time…there she was, waiting for me. She should have been long dead, a ghost as she had been before time was changed, but she wasn't. A gift from the Fates, my mother called her. They had blessed her with immortality and so, I found her again, in the most unexpected of places, in the future."

Carnick stared out at the storm, leaning back against the stone. "Your uncle had the power to control time? Do you have the ability as well? Just as you freeze time?"

"No," Ren answered, shaking his head. "In fact, my uncle had only that one time to do so, a need within the confines of the prophecy. It was something that alluded him from that point on. And I cannot change time, reverse it, or move it forward. I can freeze it, just as my father could, an ability that confounded my uncle's skills, much to his frustration."

"I'd rather have the power to move time than to freeze it."

"Would you? Would you go back? To before all of this happened? To before Xali awakened us?"

He thought for a long moment, contemplating the idea. "That's a hard decision to make. It seemed easier before this madness but now? If it brought me Xali back? I don't know."

"If it brought her back, would she still take the same steps? Return you to this same spot?"

"That blasted Elvin in you makes you like this, doesn't it? Can't just let me be content thinking I could bring her back to a happier time."

Ren laughed. "Was it truly a happier time?"

Carnick shook his head. "I don't know. She wasn't happy, never content with her status, always pushing the boundaries."

"And so it would remain that way. Taking her back would do nothing to assuage the outcome. It would still be the same."

"You're a real mood lifter, you know that?" he said sarcastically.

"So I've been told. I've also been told that my delivery of jokes leaves much to be desired."

This time, it was Carnick who laughed. "That it does!" The mood lightened, the storm outside seeming not so oppressive. He turned a blind eye to it and soaked in the feeling, enjoying Ren's company as they continued to talk. All the while the storm pounded, and Xali's fate awaited.

Xali awakened as something pulled her body swiftly from her cell. She was falling through the flames again, her skin burning with a heat that threatened to take her from consciousness once more. As fast as her cells healed, the fire scorched her, a painful blend of healing and burning that evoked a silent scream until she landed hard against the cavern floor. Her bones repaired, her fractured neck slowly reforming, the breath kicking back to her lungs in one forceful act. Coughing, she tried pulling herself up but collapsed, her body too weakened from the constant torrent of agony and repair.

She lay there, her hands gripped, lips taut with the struggle to hold back the illiquid tears. The ground shook with each footstep the god took until his shadow was over her.

"Up, Fates' tool."

She forced her head to lift and looked up at him. "Just kill me," she managed.

He let out a laugh that shook the ground once more. "Your precious Fates did this to you. She and her pet did this to you." He squatted down and picked her up by the hair, forcing her to her feet where she wobbled. "Immortality is not always a blessing."

"Why keep me alive?"

"Because you cannot be killed. You would have died on your trip down here if that were not the case. Trust me, we'd like to grant your wish, and my brothers would relish ripping you limb from limb and feasting upon your carcass."

Xali shuddered, thinking perhaps she preferred they not kill her if that were the method of doing so.

"But you can kill me. You can take my immortality, just as you tried to do to Ren."

The god spat, turning her stomach as it landed before her feet. "Do not mention the Fates' mongrel again." Something gripped her insides, cutting the breath from her and shredding her organs. They healed swiftly but not before a strangled scream escaped her.

"I am not ready to kill you yet. You will suffer for your actions, and then you will suffer more, until you are begging me for mercy, for the death that should have freed us. Even then, I will not grant it to you. You made your choice, and now you will suffer for it. A few millennia of pain may satisfy my need for vengeance, and perhaps then I will strip that touch of Orlaina's from your body and give you the death you so willingly seek."

"Were you always like this?" she dared ask, thinking the risk couldn't do her any more harm than had already come to her.

His face morphed to something terrifying, horrific enough to scare even the Dark king. Her body shook with fear, no matter how she tried to still it.

"They made us this way. Your cursed Fates. Every day since they stole this world from us, their betrayal has warped us."

"Are you certain it was their betrayal or your anger that poisoned you so?"

"She is a pertinent one, brother. Let me torment her like the other."

She hadn't realized they weren't alone and swung her head quickly to find another god sitting across the space from them, his body compacting the stones upon which he sat, his size so massive. His black eyes looked crazed as the red pupils spit long flames of fire through them. A chill ran through her, something that only brought a crooked smile to his nightmarish features.

"No, she is still their tool, and I want to know why. They gave her life, sustained with an immortality she didn't ask for, one she didn't deserve. Why?" He drew closer to Xali and roughly lifted her chin. "What is it about you that they would so freely give that kind of blessing?"

"The same you gave to Carnick? What makes me so less worthy than him?" She surprised herself at her boldness, but what did it hurt? She had nothing more to lose, and the return of her bravado gave her strength, one she'd missed as she'd lain in misery within her cell.

"He was our tool. That made him worthy."

"But why him?" The question was one she'd asked herself over and over. There were many in her family who had worshipped the gods, the elders doing so far longer than Carnick and her cousins. Why had they chosen him?

"His soul was ours from the beginning. Promised to us by his mother at your birth."

Stepping back in surprise, she tried to contain her emotion.

"She came to the temple that night and offered us his soul if we saw that the blight on their family was removed—if we dealt with the cursed child he'd been promised to, the one born under the omen of the green moons." He stepped to her, towering above her, his anger like a blanket that cloaked the space around her. Even her skin seemed to have a layer upon it. "You were ours, and Orlaina stole you from us. In return, we claimed his soul, marking it that night just as that bitch Fate did to you."

Her world spun as she contemplated his words, what Carnick's mother had done. She'd always known the niceties had been false, that she'd resented the betrothal of her son to Xali, that she'd felt tricked that he'd been given the weakest. Her words, her looks always compounding that feeling of worthlessness Xali had carried, that mark that she wasn't worthy of her son, that he'd been intended for better.

She backed away, the power of it overwhelming. She had given her only son to the gods at the same time the Mother Fate had taken Xali, both claimed, both thrown onto this path with no hesitation, no thought to the mortals whose lives they were taking, both destined to fight each other for a war that had never been theirs to fight.

"He was your weapon, and I was hers. Prophecy, destiny always there regardless of what we wanted. Why do you all feel it is your right to use us so?"

"Because you are but toys to them."

"To all of you? Carnick yours to take? My family?"

"You are creations of a greater being. You are only here because they will it so. You should be thankful we marked him, thankful we made him more than what they wanted."

"Why? What good did it do? You are still down here. I am lost to him, he to me. The Fates still have their world. What did any of it accomplish?"

"Brother, make her stop talking before I do," the other god said.

She looked around, noticing more of them had entered the space, listening to her words. She took them all in, their hardened skin, the terrifying distorted faces, bodies that towered above her, some farther than her neck allowed.

"Unless," she muttered, "unless it's not over."

The other god rose, his attention fully upon her.

"What do you mean, not over?" the one she assumed was their leader, the one who had pulled her from her cell, asked.

"You said it yourself. Why give me immortality? Why not let me die as the sacrifice that was called for?" Her hand inadvertently moved to her stomach. "There were two sacrificed that day. One still lives. They were given the sacrifice they needed." A sob escaped its prison as she said the words. "All of it led to this moment.

All so that I could live. Why?"

He studied her, contemplating her words, wondering the same as she. A hand grabbed her, large enough to encompass her entire body, and she was lifted, brought to the other god's face. "You live so that we can torture you. There is no other reason. Your Fates are cruel, crueler than we even. They left you alive to feel our wrath, knowing something needed to quell our need for revenge for the millennia we remain locked away."

He squeezed her so tight the bones began to snap, the air forced from her lungs. She screamed in agony, unable to contain it. "Stop your incessant talking, or I will step in and show you why I am the thing of nightmares."

He threw her high, her bones repairing as the flames grabbed her and led her back to her cell. She landed rough against the interior wall, her spine snapping with the force. As she lay there, feeling her cells heal the damage, she thought on her revelation. She was alive for a reason. She knew it, call it instinct as Ren called it, or something more, but she knew the Mother Fate hadn't let her die because there was more. A sacrifice had been called for, and one had been given. Her child, hers and Carnick's, sacrificed so that she could live. But to what end?

There was always a reason for everything the Fates did; she remembered the words the queen had told her. But what was the reason? Why subject her to this torture? What was she supposed to do and how when she couldn't leave this cavern or even her prison? As if to reinforce the point, the flames poured into her cell, scalding her with their touch before pulling back.

Whatever the reason, she wasn't certain she had it in her to fight for it. There was nothing left, her resolve buried under the pain and the sadness. Her strength taken from her every day with her fight just to stay conscious. She closed her eyes, thinking that perhaps she wouldn't fight any longer, not for them, not for herself, not even for Carnick. Letting his name go, she drifted, the call to disappear into the blackness of sleep too powerful.

Fourteen

The storm continued for days, battering their shield as Ren waited it out with Carnick. He'd wanted to return to his castle, to take shelter there, to hold Paige in his arms again, but Carnick refused to leave. Ren had promised himself that he would help Carnick find Xali, and so, he'd stayed.

He wondered at the storm, the sheer power of it, the lights that flashed continuously within the dark clouds. Were the Fates warring above them or were tempers simply flying? What if the Mother Fate's plan was undone, if the other Fates, the Dark Fates in particular, succeeded in changing the course of whatever path she'd lain for them? Would Xali be lost forever to them? He didn't want to think of it, wanted to think that they would find her, save her just as his father had saved his mother each time. He smiled, thinking of how his father would have corrected him, saying we saved each other Ren. It was true, there had been times when his father's life had been the one hanging in the balance, his mother coming to his rescue.

Were they up there fighting? Was his uncle by their side? And had they indeed chosen the Mother Fate's side as he suspected she'd intended? Running his hands through his hair, he stood, stretching the stiffness that had settled, feeling his cells heal the soreness of being stuck in the small space for so long a time. Carnick was sleeping, a blessing since he'd barely slept since he'd left the enclave.

Staring out into the storm, he watched the flickers of power that ran through the clouds, recognizing each as it scattered across them. They seemed to be lessening, and he couldn't draw his eyes from their patterns, watching until only a faint green could be seen. The clouds lightened, the heavy onyx color they'd born for days dissipating, until finally only a white sheen could be seen. Something had happened, something had changed.

He held his breath, worrying for the Mother Fate, for his parents, for Xali. The clouds broke, the two moons appearing, both bright and full even though they were not meant to reach their fill until many days from now. He remembered watching in amazement as they had healed after the Fates had taken back the world, but he would never forget the broken image of them that was burned into his mind from the night the war had begun.

He released his shield, breaking Carnick's down as well, and walked closer to the ledge. The wind was warm against his skin where it had been cold and bitter just moments prior. A soft breeze ruffled his hair, accompanied by the smell of lilac, and he smiled, his heart at peace again.

Ren, his mother's voice called through his mind.

Mother, you're safe.

A light laugh trickled through his head. *And you think your father would have it any other way?*

No, I suppose I should know better. Is the Mother Fate?

Your path is still a clear one, Ren. All is well, she is stronger than any of them realized. Why the men in this world continue to doubt the power of their women is beyond me.

He laughed. *I've been taught better.*

You have, and Paige will remind you of it should you ever forget. Now hurry, you've much to traverse before your journey is complete.

Will you be with me?

No. The sadness of her voice was palpable. *I am needed elsewhere. I made a promise, and I have been gone too long.*

Xali. So, she does live.

Shhh. All will be revealed in time. Stay by his side and do not waver. You are still a part of this, Ren. His part has been played, but yours and Xali's are still in motion.

His heart dropped. The elation he'd had at her confirmation that Xali lived ripped away with her words.

The breeze drifted over his face as he heard, *I love you, Ren.*

"I love you, too, Mother," he said aloud, having felt her pull away from his mind.

"Do you often call the air mother and tell it you love it?" Carnick said behind him, taking him from his peaceful place.

"When my mother is the wind, then yes," he answered with a slight laugh, his mother's words still heavy in his chest.

"Your mother. She was here?"

"In spirit." He breathed in the lilac that lingered on the breeze.

"Then the war among the Fates is over?"

"Aye, and it is time once again to turn our eyes to the mountains and find Xali."

Carnick wasted no time, beginning his ascent as if the last few days of stasis had not occurred.

"Are you certain shifting wouldn't be the wiser thing?" he asked, knowing the answer.

Carnick shot him a look. "Why do you ask when you know my response? Aren't you supposed to have some special instinct about things?"

Shaking his head, Ren gave one last glance to the east where the stars shone again in the clear sky and followed Carnick, knowing there would be no swaying him from trudging forward, no matter how arduous the task.

The noise of the relentless flames echoed through the caverns, crashing repeatedly into Xali's cell. She'd been there since the gods had thrown her back, unable to move, unable to will herself to even lift her head. Ainia had come once more to bring her food, saying barely anything, simply setting her sad eyes on Xali's before rushing away. The food sat where she'd left it, untouched.

After she'd been returned to her prison, the epiphany she'd had earlier returned to her, the truth of it, the raw insensitivity of it, gnawing at her. There had been a sacrifice that day: her son. An innocent child, yet unborn to meet his full potential, murdered at the hands of the Fates. Of the Mother Fate. She'd refused to believe it at first, but it was the only explanation for the life that still flowed through her veins. A sacrifice of her blood had been required to imprison the gods or free them. Her child was of her blood and so the prison had been sealed once again, the gods ripped from their goal of vengeance and banished to their prison once more.

It angered her, the loss and the deception, and that anger numbed her pain. She felt deceived by the Mother Fate, used, a tool in a war she'd never wanted, one that had been theirs to fight, not hers. The more she stewed, the greater her anger until it overcame all else. She sensed the stir of the Darkness in her as it rose to answer her ire.

She was about to embrace it, to let it overtake the nature side when the air stirred, just slightly enough for her to sense it, a cool touch upon her skin. The anger and then the pain below subsided for just that moment, and she breathed fully.

Shhh, she heard the queen's voice in her head. *I promised I would not leave you. I am here.*

"Help me," she whispered hoarsely as the faint scent of lilac awoke her senses, forgetting for that moment the anger she'd held only moments before.

I have no power over their domain, that is the work of the Dark Fates. The Mother Fate cannot enter, nor can I.

Then how are you speaking to me?

With great effort and help from my husband, now hush and listen. The same strength that runs through me is within you. That is why we are connected. It comes from the Mother Fate and is something others do not often recognize. That is why we are tested and survive the test.

But she deceived me. She murdered my son, took him from me before I could even hold him. Sacrificed for her war.

A son that was never meant to be, child. You are meant to carry a female heir. You know that in your heart.

But the child—

Was never to be. It was a false child, a soul now safe in the Mother Fate's care, borrowed to serve a purpose.

A tool, just as I was.

As we all are. I prefer to call us players, all serving a greater purpose, one I told you would not be realized until you were free of your path. You will bear another, Xaliandri, and she will be strong and brave just as you are because you sacrificed for her.

Tears burned behind her eyes but still did not fall, her tear ducts too dry to bring them to fruition. *Just as your sacrifices strengthened Ren.*

Yes, everything we persevered was for him, and I would suffer through all of it again for him, just as you will one day say the same.

No, I will never escape this prison, not without your help.

Hush, you will survive this, overcome it, and face the truth. Look inside yourself, find the tie to the Mother Fate, she is your creator, your salvation just as she was mine.

But how do I do that when I can barely move, barely breathe even?

No answer came for a long while, and Xali felt the absence of the queen. Then the queen's voice faintly touched her mind again, saying only, *Search for the emerald water, Xali.*

The last words came as a whisper on the wind, fading with her presence once more, leaving Xali alone and strangely cold. The pain remained, but it was more of a discomfort, the queen having diminished it with her mere presence. The anger had dissipated completely, as if it had never been.

Xali lay there, thinking on her words wondering why she'd been a sacrifice, why the queen had been one. The females always meant to carry the burden of prophecy. She supposed the Mother Fate had carried her own. Xali wondered at her story, knowing only parts but thinking the whole was likely the show of a woman who was tormented at every turn through actions of the men who claimed to love her.

Staring at the flames that surrounded her cell, she wondered at the Mother Fate's own strength. Was that what she'd imbued in Xali and the queen? The strength to persevere in even the worst of situations, to overcome them, to turn them to her own advantage. A prophecy that would heal the wrongs against her, her people, her lover.

Lifting her head, she closed her eyes and did as the queen had said, searching for that part of her that came from the Mother Fate, not the magic which been absent since her fall, but the inner power. She pulled herself to a sitting position and relaxed completely, pushing aside the remaining pain and looking far inward.

A calm overtake her, one that poured through her body. It was set with determination and fortitude she could feel stirring in her blood, and so she called it, letting it take over everything else she was feeling, becoming one with it.

Opening her eyes, she could see the cooling black parts of the flames, sense the presence of the land, severed and violated by the prison the Dark Fates had created, feel the imbalance of power that was like a soft undercurrent. She reached to it, noticing the subtle differences of that power, the beauty it had once held that now had been warped and turned. The beauty that had once been the gods. It drifted over her, her own nature magic, the Elvin part of her, returning, reaching for it, feeling the connection.

They were compatible just as the nature and Dark were. The magic tingled upon her skin, reminding her of Carnick then of her family, for it was their magic as well, magic the gods had imbued upon their line for their millennia of worship and dedication, pushing the Darkness below, in a way overtaking it to become the dominant power alongside the nature. There was a beautiful violence to it, one that was similar to the Dark, easy to confuse they were so alike.

Time and influence had changed her family, reshaping their magic, allowing the gods easy control of them, but also making them the gods' children, stealing them from the Mother Fate and her lover the day her people had been cast out, the day her family had turned its back on its true creators and accepted a new one.

Xali was the only one who held the original magic, in its unmanipulated form because the Mother Fate had claimed her the night of her birth, damned her for a prophecy. But why? If joining the people, waking the immortals had not been the final intent but only a step toward its fruition, what was the goal? What was it she was meant to do?

In answer, the nature in her rose to meet the gods' power that tingled along her skin, the vibrant green turning a royal blue that swirled before her eyes, the two powers forming a beautiful helix that twisted, parts of it empty like it awaited other pieces. Xali scrambled back as it hit her. The merging of all four powers. And she was the key to bringing it to fruition. But how? How did she bring peace to those who didn't seek it?

Or perhaps some of them did. Some, like the Mother Fate.

She is your creator, your salvation, the queen's words echoed through her head. She was a child of the Mother Fate. Chosen by her when no other had been. Xali stood, calling her nature magic back, letting it merge once again with the Dark, letting the nature take the lead. Whatever she needed to do, she had to get to the water, it had been fiery red, but she knew it had once run green, connected to all the other water that flowed through the Elvin Enclave.

Her power had been absent until now, and she pondered if it had been the gods' doing or her own. Had it been present this entire time, yet buried below her emotions? Whatever the reason, it was back. Could she shift? If so, she didn't think she could shift beyond the gods' prison, she could feel the slight weight of the Fates' magic far above her. It was a risk. If they caught her, they would punish her, but they had been punishing her, so was there any difference? Her mind wandered to Sartria, her small body brutally pinned below the brute god who had claimed her, and a shiver ran through her. Yes, it could get worse, but this was her path, and she needed to follow it, no matter the consequence.

Closing her eyes, she thought of the place the god had taken her, momentarily contemplating his reason for taking her there. Had he known? Had he once felt the Mother Fate's presence there?

Focus, Xali, she told herself, clearing her head.

She concentrated on the small cave, then remembering how Ren had told her the Dark part of her powered her shifts, she let her anger free, feeling it rise from deep within her. Anger at being the sacrifice, at the loss of her child for that sacrifice, at Carnick's possession, at all the wasted lives for a petty war over one woman. The anger boiled over, and she clung to it as the magic of the cavern took form. Her feet were groundless for a split second, then it was below her again, the gentle lapping of water filling her ears.

She opened her eyes, the cavern surrounding her. The water remained red and angry, and she remembered the feel of it as it had scalded her skin. Uncertain of what she was meant to find, she looked around, praying the gods didn't discover her before she found whatever her purpose was for being here.

Purpose.

Find the green water.

That had been the purpose, but the water wasn't green. What was she supposed to do? She paced, knocking her fist to her head, worry seeping in, doubt, and with it the pain climbed. It had been quiet when she'd been determined but now as her determination wavered, her purpose unclear again, it roared, throwing her to the ground and tearing through her.

How had they found her?

She writhed on the floor, biting her lip hard to keep from screaming, the pain searing through her viciously, immobilizing her. Her eyes stared vacantly at the cavern wall as her strength left her and agony replaced it.

Remember who you are, the queen's voice drifted through her mind.

There was a tiny shimmer in the wall, and she fixed her eyes to it, trying to hold onto the calming of the queen's voice, but the pain was overwhelming.

It's supposed to be, she said to herself.

It was a prison. An internal prison, binding her magic, her spirit, her strength.

Remember who you are.

She was different, special, her powers only a recent part of her. The strength had been there from an early age. The need to prove herself, to be the strongest of her cousins even without magic. A fire burned within her, one that came from her constant struggle, that constant fight to be Carnick's equal, to be seen as something more than broken, more than the bad omen that had cursed her family. An inner strength that, try as they might, could not be broken. That was who she was and her connection to the Mother Fate, always seen as less, fed that strength and determination. Fed the uniqueness that was her.

With her realization, the pain subsided. She was strong. They wouldn't hold her back, she would beat this, find her purpose, and free herself from this prison. Her fingers moved, and she willed herself to stretch her hand out toward the wall. The emerald shimmer grew, slowly revealing an emerald stone, its light shining upon her, cutting the darkness, spreading to other stones that began to sparkle, emerald and onyx then a brilliant blue the color of Ren's eyes. The Fates had once been here. The blues and blacks over-took the emerald and Xali saw the story, the helplessness of the Mother Fate to save her friends, the men she'd known from wher-ever they'd come from, helpless to stop the jealousy and fear that ran through the others.

She hadn't cursed them here, she had tried to stop it, just as she had tried to save Xali's people. The emerald began to sparkle again, slowly overtaking the other stones until the cavern glowed green, the magic calling to her own, the pain subsiding as she saw the purpose. She was the carrier of the burden, the redemption of the Mother Fate to the gods. Her nature power soared within, the magic from the stones strengthening her, fortifying her as she pulled herself to her feet.

With her magic around her, and that of the Mother Fate, she stepped into the water, expecting it to scald her, but instead it cooled at her touch, the emerald spreading to it with each step until it cast itself further than Xali's eyes could see. A peace fell upon her as a quake rumbled through the prison. The first step had been taken.

She heard yelling, and the god appeared but at the edge of the cavern as if he couldn't enter. She turned to face him, feeling the power of the Mother Fate within her.

"Orlaina," he said softly before his demeanor changed.

He sent his power toward her, and she put her hand out, know-ing she would stop it. It hung in the air, and then she called to it just as she had earlier, feeling the beauty of its strength, the intri-cate blend of magic that felt Dark but not quite. There was a fire to it that warmed her skin, vibrant ribbons of red edged with ebony that danced around her in slow motion.

She held her hand out to them, feeling the tingle of their unique magic as it grazed her fingertips. Then she pulled her hands up, drawing the ribbons forth, and casting them to the walls of the cave. The ebony, cerulean, and onyx stones shone bright in ribbons of their own that danced among the god's power. The sight was entrancing, the cavern glowing with the power that faded slowly as she let the tendrils drop to the ground, silver and gold shimmers all that remained.

She looked to the god whose eyes were wide with disbelief. Bravely, she approached him. He stood not in his man form but the beast he had become, the beast his former brethren had turned him to with time in a prison that should never have been. With no hesitation, she placed a hand on him, watching as the worn, creviced leathered arm morphed to a soft glowing skin.

"Jealousy, mistrust, and greed left you here, turning you to anger and hatred, hiding the beauty of who you and your brothers truly are. She tried to save you, but the others were too blind, and their power buried her cries. You were her friend, her brother, and for loving her, you were cursed. For that harm, she has sent me."

Glorious eyes of silver shone brightly, red flickers within, evaluating her, his hair of gold lit with silver fell to his shoulders, the silver seeming to sparkle the closer it came to his eyes. Golden. His hair was golden, like that of the Elvin. Had the Mother Fate created her people with a nod to the ones who had been lost? Or, had she once held hair of gold, closer to these gods than to the Fates she called her family? It couldn't have been coincidence, and she wondered at the significance, wondered as well if it was something to which she would ever find the answer.

The god looked down at his hand, hers seeming so tiny until he transformed to the stature of a man and took her hand, studying the fragileness of it, for even in mortal form he was a formidable size.

He grasped her hand, holding it tight but not harming her. His eyes lifted back to hers as the feel of the Mother Fate faded, her power with it, leaving Xali feeling weak for just that moment. But she wasn't weak, and the Dark in her rose to challenge that feeling, pushing at the nature to show itself in force or risk being overruled by the Dark. That determination she'd had before returned and with it the feel of her magic within her veins, ebbing and flowing as a tide that moved within her, stronger she noted than it had ever felt.

"You have freed us," the god said, making no mention of the internal change within her.

She shook her head. "No, not quite. Only returned you to what you once were. A reminder, I think, from her."

"A reminder of what? And what good does that do if we are still trapped here?" She could hear the anger, the red in his eyes growing.

"A reminder of who you once were…" She paused, thinking on his question. Why the change? What did it do if it made no difference? Or perhaps it would.

"In preparation for your return? I think…well I'm not sure, but I think my death, the death of my child was the sacrifice to make amends."

He pulled her hand away.

"Amends? The death of an unborn child is nothing. You didn't die. You live still! There has been no amends. The death was to seal this prison again and nothing more."

He stormed off, returning to his overwhelming size. Xali chased after him, her mind trying to figure it out, to fit all the pieces into place. What was she missing?

She stopped, the eyes of each god upon her, all of them with that same shocked look, all now glorious like the Fates. What would they do to her if she didn't find the answer?

Her eyes fell to the corner where Sartria lay, staring in disbelief at the former beasts, her naked body trembling in fear. Their eyes met, the eyes of a broken woman to a strong defiant one. Sartria had been possessed by the gods, their power corrupting her as it had Carnick but that power, where had it come from? Had the connection always been there, or had it developed over time? Carnick's mother had sacrificed him but what about the rest of them?

"The magic the others possess, part of it comes from you, doesn't it?"

They stared at her.

"Why? Why does your power run through the veins of my family?" she demanded.

"Because your ancestors invited it."

She couldn't help but stare at him, not fully comprehending.

"They were angry, and we took that anger, whispering to them of another choice, another god who wouldn't abandon them as your precious Fates had done. We could feel their desperation through the land, their need for something to cling to, we provided it and they took it. Drakine was the first to ask for more."

"Drakine? The great king?"

"Ha! Great only because we gave him the means. He offered his soul and that of every generation following for power, not satisfied with what he'd been given. He prayed to us as your people had since the day they were cast aside. And with each prayer, our connection to them, to your family grew. When he offered to be ours, to turn from the Fates forever, to avenge us in avenging his people, we gifted him."

"Drakine sold his own flesh and blood for power?"

"Yes, we manipulated the gifts the Fates had given him, them none the wiser, having forgotten your people, too concerned about their precious chosen ones, their sight blind to all else."

Xali was dumbfounded, her take on everything thrown on its head. They'd all been wrong, the gods of her people really were these gods and not some false gods, not some confused term for the Fates. These gods had changed the course of her people, of her family and become their deity. They'd offered Drakine exactly what he'd wanted, what all of her ancestors had wanted, revenge and a way to enact it.

"You gave him the spell to undo the immortals."

He laughed, a sound that echoed through the space. "Yes, those precious children of the Fates. Taken down so easily. Then we waited, knowing we needed just the right sacrifice to undo the Fates completely."

"Me."

"You. Orlaina claimed your soul the night you were born, thinking she was helping, that you would bring about our demise and protect her children, but she was wrong."

A soft breeze brushed her loose hair, the warmth different than that of the queen's, its touch familiar, one she remembered from her youth when she'd been alone in the fields outside her palace, the same one that had driven her to first climb the guardian wall and look upon the forests beyond. A breeze that shouldn't have been deep in the belly of a mountain prison.

"No," she said softly, knowing the Mother Fate was sending her a sign. "She claimed me to free you."

He raised a brow, and the others laughed.

"Let's go back to torturing her, I've grown bored of talk, Fioch."

He raised a hand to quiet them.

"We are her people, too," she said defiantly.

"Thrown aside, alone without her. You are no longer her people. You stopped being her people the day she abandoned you with the rest of the Fates."

"She didn't have a choice, just as she had none with your imprisonment. They overpowered her, they dismissed her, just as they always did, just as they dismissed all of her children, both the Elvin and my people. Something has changed, her sway is greater, her power greater. I am proof of that. Dismissed as well by my family, by you, seen as nothing all these years. Just as the queen was, her power seen as less when it is not less, it never was. The queen proved that to the other immortals and…and I'm here to prove it to you. I am her amends, her hand out to you extended in peace."

He stepped closer, towering over her but she stood tall, unwavering. "She had the chance when we broke free."

"When you persuaded my aunts to kill me? Her child? Then viciously attacked the land, her land? You were too angry, too out for revenge and destruction. I…I was sacrificed so that you were given the chance to see that she is ready." She touched his hand.

"Her power runs through me. She brought you back to what you once were."

"And the others? The thieves who stole this world from us? What do they want? They are a jealous, angry lot, and I guarantee neither Diarmund nor Aodhan want us to resurface, neither wanting us anywhere near Orlaina."

She drew her hand back, unsure of the answer. She wasn't even certain who Aodhan and Diarmund were but assumed one was Orlaina's lover, the other his brother.

"She doesn't know," one of the gods yelled. "She is ignorant of our past, even of the Fates she claims loyalty to."

"And you don't even know how to get us out of here," he said to her.

They all turned away, and that grip of their power choked her, pulling her, its intent to relegate her to her cell once more, but something rose within her, a desperate need to persuade them. The grip remained, pain trying to tear at her strength. It angered her, being dismissed once again. She would not be sent away; she would no longer cower to their brutality. They would listen to her whether they wanted to hear her words or not. She was certain she was right, that she was the key to all of this, that she could help.

Her power rose, and she grabbed his power, throwing it out so that it rebounded against them all. They turned ready to attack.

"I am tired of being dismissed!" she yelled. "I am not some weak child!"

"But you are no god."

"No, but I'm more than you choose to see, I'm more than anyone has ever chosen to see, only Carnick saw me, and you chose to torment him for it. I'm tired of not being seen or heard!"

As the words left her mouth, she pushed her hands out, the ground below erupting, flowers and roots breaking through where nothing should have grown, her power exploding. She gave herself over to the magic, the emotion feeding it.

"My powers are not weak, nor have they ever been. The magic

of the Mother Fate, of Orlaina, flows through my veins because I am her child, her chosen weapon to undue all that was done when you first fell, when you morphed to the beasts of vengeance, when you insinuated yourselves into the lives of my people and the power of my family."

A root reached out and she grabbed it, the magic overtaking her. She jumped to a ledge, the flowers appearing as her feet hit it, crashing down in waves of the magic that was pouring from her. She ran, as if music within her drove her actions, with each step, each touch, the surroundings morphed. She leapt down, running through them, the emerald of her power cascading through the space. Reaching the cavern, she called to the water which heeded her command, rising then rushing with a force through the center of the open space. Flowing up in a wave to the top of the prison, causing chunks of rock to fall upon them.

The gods didn't move, continuing to stare at her as she transformed their volcanic home to a paradise.

Water rained in droplets upon her as she ran to Sartria and picked her up, clothing her in a dress of peonies.

"I forgive you," she whispered to Sartria.

She heard grumbling from one of the gods, but it was stayed as Xali swept her hand out and a sea of grass rose from under their feet. She kissed her cousin's cheek then ran, grabbing another root and continued to cast her magic, the feel exhilarating, like nothing she'd ever experienced. Finally in one giant bound, she leapt from the root, the prison quaking with her landing.

Around her, a beautiful garden of plants and colors she'd never seen flourished. It was a paradise. The emerald water, continued to flow upward in a cascading motion that resembled a backwards waterfall, churning against the upper levels of the cavern that held them, trying to break free. Where it met the flames, steam swirled around it, the flames unable to stop its flow but continuing their burn, whatever invisible fuel that drove it constant.

A few drops of emerald water dripped upon her arm as she

caught her breath, taking in the transformation that had occurred from her hands. No, from the magic of the Mother Fate that had yet to fade from her core. She sensed it there, pulsing with a steady rhythm, alive within her.

She turned her eyes from the emerald water to the gods. There was silence as they looked around, taking in the new world that encompassed them. The pounding of the waterfall the only sound, the prior rumbling of the cavern having quieted.

They turned to her in silence until the leader finally spoke to her.

"This is what our land once looked like, what we built when we created it. We didn't have the same abilities as Orlaina, but she'd given me something when we left, a reminder of her, and when I opened it, this is what was created, a world that spoke of her but that was remarkably us. We are not gentle, soft gods like the Light gods, like she can be."

"Not when she's moody, Fioch."

"She is feisty when she's angered." He looked around then back at Xali. "Perhaps she is sending us something through you after all, child."

"But what, Fioch? This did nothing but shower us with rock and move the ground some," the one who had claimed Sartria said, ripping a handful of flowers from the new terrain. "Flowers do us no good. They do nothing but remind us of what we once had."

It was true, but the water was still flowing upward, and the prison had shaken with a mighty force. A sign perhaps? But of what?

"Or to whom," she mumbled.

"What?"

"Maybe I'm not the one who is bound to free you. Maybe I am only a key, one player," she said, using the word the queen had favored, "among three. Two of us have played our parts, and one remains. One key left, and now the door must be opened."

"By us?"

She thought about it. Was she right? All of the strife that had occurred since she'd woken the immortals. The changes that had been brought about by her actions had laid a foundation for this moment. She and Carnick tied to Ren in a prophecy he had seen firsthand. Carnick's role had been played, bringing her to this point, the impetus to her presence in the prison of the gods, to her immortality, to the additional magic that now pulsed through her body like a gentle wave. But Ren's role was not so clear. He had been made witness to Carnick's transformation, to the violence that had ensued. He had been witness to her sacrifice, he likely the one who had pulled Carnick from that ledge that day as they'd watched her fall, one who was now continuing to hold him up. His role, however, was not clear, it never had been to any of them. Never as prominent as hers and Carnick's had been. Perhaps not until now.

"No, by Ren. There were two of us in that prophecy, or maybe all three of our names were written there. I am not the only player here."

"That mutt of the Fates is who will free us? I highly doubt that."

"He's not a mutt. He's a mix of all three powers, a joining of all the Fates."

"A mutt. Diluting their power to what end?"

"To peace among them and this, my people, you, are the last step in that. The Fates undoing the wrongs against the woman they all loved, against those who loved her. Ren is not diluted power, he's a force to be reckoned with…just as Carnick was. You made Carnick and Drakine into the same thing, mingling your powers with that of the Mother Fate and the Dark Fate. All three now housed in Carnick, if his power remains."

"Yes. I had intended to strip him of his power as we fell, but I decided against it. I left him as is, a warning to your foolish Fates, a reminder to Orlaina of me."

"And you made him into the same as Ren. A symbol of harmony. You merged the powers the same as they did, whether that was your intention or not."

His silver eyes evaluated her, their weight almost crushing. She could see him thinking it through, making sense of her words, just as she was letting them settle in her mind, the revelation a powerful one. With it, the thought of the child, the one the queen had told her was yet to come. A blending now not only of their magic as it had once been, a delicate balance between Dark and Elvin, but now the additional magic within Carnick passing to their child. She prayed she would live to bear that child for now she understood. The child would be born to an immortal mother. Did Carnick remain immortal? If so, would their daughter's birth come as Ren's son's did? A final blending of all the powers into one final heir. Two paths of a prophecy merged to become that child.

The power of the thought was enough to make her take a step back, her hands shaking. For it meant more than simply a child with four streams of magic, it meant that free will had never been theirs, any of theirs. Not the queen's nor the Dark king's, not his brother's, not Ren's, or even hers. Every step of their lives had been orchestrated down to the very bruises and tears shed by her and the queen, to the pain the Dark king had born, to the pain Carnick now bore with her absence. All purposeful, paths drawn out and manipulated by the Mother Fate to an end that celebrated all that she loved. Her people, the immortals, the other Dark Fates, the Light Fates, and the gods.

As if he'd read her thoughts, the god shook his head. "She was always stronger than any of them chose to see, only Diarmund saw it, but Aodhan was blind to it, as were the others. And she let them remain that way, content in knowing her own strength, never one to flaunt it like Aodhan. He hated me because I embraced her strength, encouraged her to use it, to stand up to him and the others." He was quiet for a moment. "And now she has shown it, but to what end? To force the hand of all of us and blend our powers whether we like it or not?"

"Yes, because only in doing so does she show that you are all brothers, as I think you may have once been, long before jealousy, greed, and the love of a woman destroyed it all."

Fifteen

Carnick was exhausted. They'd searched for days after the storms, but found no sign of Xali or an entrance to where the gods were being held. Nothing, even with the help of Ren's men. They were no closer to finding her than when they'd started.

"Carnick," he heard Ren say but ignored him, not wanting to hear the words he knew he was about to say. Not wanting to give up.

"Carnick, we need to take a break, go back, rest, reformulate a plan."

"No, I won't leave until we have her."

Ren grabbed him. "We need to go back. We've found nothing, and the weather is worsening. There's another storm coming, and I can't tell if it's natural or something more that's brewing again with the Fates. We don't know that their feud isn't starting once more."

He was right, storm clouds had rolled in, the sky dark and gray, even with the full moons above. The snow had been relentless since that morning and was worsening.

"No, can't you use your power to stop the storm?"

"It doesn't work that way, especially if this is the work of the Fates. Carnick, you haven't slept in days."

"And I won't sleep until I have her back."

He turned his back on Ren, hearing his sigh, even below the sound of the wind. The storm quieted suddenly, and he turned back to thank Ren, thinking he'd somehow calmed it, but the mountain shook, knocking him over with its force.

"What in the Fates?" Ren said, helping him up.

"You didn't do that?"

"No."

They both looked around as the sky cleared, the snow lightening.

"That storm was increasing in strength, why is it stopping now?" Ren asked.

"I thought you calmed it."

"No, that is not my doing."

Water began to trickle down the side of the mountain, a bright green that sparkled in the moonlight.

Carnick met Ren's eyes. "What's happening?"

"I don't know." Ren stooped to touch the water. "It's the same that runs through the enclave, as though the two are connected."

"But what does it mean?"

A faraway look crossed Ren's face, his eyes turning to match the color of the water. Carnick didn't know what to do, and afraid to say anything, he stayed silent. All the while, his heart had begun to hammer in his chest. Something was happening, he was sure of it, and the wait for Ren's focus, for whatever revelation he was about to have, was torturous. He felt helpless being forced to wait, a weak feeling that caused his Dark side to rise in an attempt to defeat that weakness. With it, that foreign feeling, the power of the gods that had not been removed, rumbled deep within him.

The air seemed to still as Carnick watched, and his power brewed like the storm that had swirled around them. After what seemed an eternity, but was likely only a few uncomfortable moments, Ren focused, the green succumbing to the blue his eyes typically held.

"Ren?"

"Mother, she says to listen."

"Listen? To what?"

Ren looked around, then his eyes followed where the water trailed to puddle before them.

"Not to what, to whom. That quake, the water, it's Xali."

Carnick was dumbstruck as Ren made his way to the ledge below them, standing next to the puddle. That's when Carnick noticed that the ledge below was more of a crevice, the mountain spreading wide below it compared to where he stood, this side of the mountain distinctly narrowing. It gave the appearance that the mountain was split at that point, separating into two peaks. Why hadn't they noticed this before?

He was about to call Ren's attention to it when he heard a sharp crack and the water, along with Ren disappeared, swallowed below as the ledge buckled.

Ren, listen, his mother's voice had called. What had she meant? Ren stared at the water that had pooled. If the quake and the water were Xali's doing, what did that tell him? Something was going on in the prison that couldn't be found, something important. Something upon which their future rested. The quieting of the storm told him this much, the touch of his mother's voice confirming it.

He stared at the water, noticing how it pooled, how there seemed a distinction between the two parts of the mountain they were currently nestled within. A connection to the two, like they had once been separated. He was about to tell Carnick this when the ground buckled below him, pulling him under with the water.

His instinct was to shift out of the fall, but something told him that wasn't what he was meant to do. Instead, he let himself fall, the water surrounding him in droplets until the heat became unbearable and they dissipated. He fought the urge to flee as flames licked his skin, his cells repairing with each intrusion. The Dark in him tolerated the pain, reveling in it.

At some point, he felt the resistance of the Fates' magic, a barrier below the prison boundary. It pushed at his skin like he was an invader it needed to repel, but then, as if recognizing him, it gave, and he continued his descent. The air turned, that distinct foreign power invading his senses, his eyes catching colors, his power reacting to the feel of Xali's magic and another—the Mother Fate's.

He sensed ground below and prepared himself, landing with a thunder that rippled the ground, his body crouched, ready to protect itself. He looked up, spying Xali's feet, relief sweeping over him, then he spotted the gods. They weren't the same gods that had been the things of nightmares. These were similar to the Fates, their eyes and hair the only distinction. Hair the golden of his mothers, of the Elvin. Had that characteristic been a coincidence or was it something more? Quickly, he stood, letting the thought go and drawing his power even though he knew he stood no chance against the gods.

"Ren!" Xali yelled, running to him. She was stopped mid-run as the god closest to her grabbed her with his power.

Ren could see the momentary pain in her eyes and was about to strike when she did something remarkable. She turned the power from her. He could see it morphing as a ribbon-like substance that played upon her skin. She turned to face the god and flung the magic back at him, knocking him a step backward. He seemed impressed rather than angry.

"I told you I was tired of being underestimated."

"I think I've missed something," Ren said, still in a defensive stance.

"You certainly did," she said.

"Fates' favored mutt, have they sent you as sacrifice?" one of the gods growled.

Ren bristled at the word mutt but said nothing.

"Why would they send you here?" the one nearest Xali asked.

"I don't know, but they did." He looked around, taking in the beauty of the space, the abundance of flora, the stream of emerald water that coursed through it. He followed its source, feeling the current of power. "For some reason, they want me here," he answered gruffly.

"You are the lifeline," Xali said.

He turned to her, noting now the emerald that danced within the gray storm clouds of her eyes. She carried a confidence that came with experience, with knowledge, with having suffered. It was the same air his mother had carried so elegantly. He could feel there was no longer a second soul within her, it's death a brutal part of the Fates' plan. Perhaps, she had accepted the same fact, owning it and letting it embolden her.

"There are three of us on the path. Carnick has played his part, and now the rest is up to us," she continued. "She turned her back to the gods. The Mother Fate. We are a gesture of peace, a chance for the Fates to make it right," she looked to the gods, "for you to take your rightful place aboveground at their side."

"Their side?" a god said. "We created this world, it is ours."

"No longer. They took the foundation you laid and enhanced it, giving it life, like you never did. There are races of people up there, ones which bear your mark."

Ren listened as she spoke, her words powerful. Did she know what he and Carnick had discovered? Her true place in all this? Ushering in a new immortal line? Upon that thought, he noticed her aura, distinctly immortal, like Carnick. The Mother Fate had blessed her when she'd given herself to her destiny and taken the leap to save them. She wore the immortality as if it had always been hers to own.

"A people ruled by the Fates and this mutt."

Ren grew hot. "I am not a mutt, and some of those people are yours. They pray to you, worship you, not the Fates, not their creators. It is you to whom they bow. Carnick and Xali rule those people, not I, and one day, their daughter will rule alongside my son, the two bringing the power of the gods and the Fates together finally."

Xali turned quickly to look at him. "You know?"

So, she, too, had figured it out. "Yes, there will be another to replace the one sacrificed. The Fates have a reason for everything they do, especially the Mother Fate."

There was a sadness to her eyes, a grief that only came with the loss of an unborn child, one she would carry her entire life. She replaced it quickly with that confidence that he'd seen earlier, giving him a nod before turning back to the gods.

"She is handing you an offering of peace. She has swayed them," Xali said to the gods. "She has finally made them see their wrong, and this is her solution. Do you accept? Will you walk above the ground, take the people with which you have been charged? Accept a new role in the future of our world?"

There was grumbling from the gods, and Ren noticed the shift in the air, their power encompassing the space. The silver in the eyes of the one who appeared to be their leader morphed to a liquidlike motion that was similar to the way the storm clouds swayed in Xali's and Carnick's eyes.

"Share? What is rightfully ours?"

They seemed to grow in size, angry, violent, lashing out at Ren and Xali. Ren was thrown back with the force, his spine fracturing as it took the brunt of the impact against the cavern wall. He clawed his way to a crouched position as the broken vertebrae healed.

"We will not cower to those who betrayed us!" the god roared. The cavern shook, pieces of rock pelting them.

Ren searched for Xali, she'd fallen and was pinned beneath the hand of another god who was holding her tight. All confidence she'd had was gone as she struggled to grasp her power and free herself. Even with all she held, she had trouble harnessing it when she was in dire straits.

The god's power grasped him, and Ren was pulled to him with a force that knocked the air from his lungs. He knew better than to fight back, knowing it would be his death, remembering the way the immortality had fled his body the last time the god had set his sights on him. He looked up at the massive being, feeling small for the first time in his life, powerless for only the second.

The god studied him. "Why should I not kill you as I intended the first time I saw you?"

"Because she sent me to you."

"As a sacrifice like the girl? Some sacrifice. She lives still."

"Because you let her live. You have the power to kill her just as you do me. Why have you not killed her?"

"Ren? What are you doing?" Xali yelled.

"Because she needed to suffer and suffer she will," the god replied, ignoring her.

The other gods nodded in agreement, and Xali was picked up by an unseen force as the hand holding her released her. Flames enshrouded her body, and he could hear her screams.

"No!" he yelled, struggling against the grip that had him. Something in him triggered with the sight; all the stories of the torment his mother had endured, the trauma she and his father had faced, the wrongs righted through their sacrifice, came to the surface. Xali was just another pawn in a game that had nothing to do with any of them, and he was tired of seeing those he cared about hurt from the games the Fates played. All at the hands of the Mother Fate, manipulating the lives of her children, the ones she deemed special, her chosen. Chosen to give their souls, their lives to her agenda, to fix whatever it was she could never fix. He was tired of the pain he'd seen in his mother's eyes, the burden his father had carried, the rift it had caused them in their first life, carried over for millennia. A burden which they'd never asked to carry, the same Xali had never asked to take.

The powers in him collided as they never had before, the three intertwining with a force that pushed him from the god's hand. He landed low, his hand to the ground as he brought his eyes up to meet the god's. His power swirled around him in a violet haze that filled the space, eclipsing that of the gods. It seeped from his eyes, eyes he knew were a vibrant violet that matched his power.

"There will be no more sacrifice, no more harm to innocents who are not part of this fight, who are not part of the game the Fates play, of the quarrels they have, the guilt they hold. No more will come from those I love, those under my protection. This ends now."

The god evaluated him, the silver in his eyes lightening. The flames around Xali dissipated, and her body dropped to the ground, the charred skin healing as she lifted her eyes to Ren. "It's your move," she mouthed.

And he knew she was right. All of it coming to this moment. "I am not a mutt, I am a blend of three lines of Fates, a unifying of the powers they hold. A symbol of all they struggled to create when they made this world atop the one you created. I am formidable, whether you think so or not, with purpose." He took a step forward. "I, like my parents before me, am a version of the Fates themselves, a Fate incarnate with the power to stop you or to help you."

"You stop us?" the one who'd held Xali snarled.

Xali had risen and answered his question, moving to stand beside Ren as she did, "The two of us."

"You cannot even stop the flames that eat your flesh, and you want me to believe you will help him? He may be a formidable opponent, one who has yet to reach his full potential, but may have just unleashed it." The god moved his hand through the violet power that still hung in the air, Ren never standing down. "But you—"

"Hold the power of the Mother Fate within me. I just failed to embrace it as I should have, to own it as mine, thinking it simply a borrowed power, lent to me in a time of need. She is my true mother, blessing me with the magic needed to stand beside Ren."

"Orlaina has abused you, tormented you, and from the sound of this one, done the same to those he cherishes. Why stand for her after all she has done to you?"

It was Ren who answered, seeing now the true purpose of it all, his anger abated, the calm of his mother's blood rising to clear his sight. "Because true prophecy is the hardest to bear, we children of prophecy must carry the burden of it, be tested by it, all to be strengthened by it, to see that it is fulfilled. My parents understood this, I now do as well. Xaliandri is your salvation, the one who will lead you to the freedom you desire and the ability to be the true gods of the people the Mother Fate gave you when she sent them away." As the words left his mouth, he saw the truth of them. She had known, not only begging for her people's lives but knowing they would find the gods and raise them from the prison where they'd been cursed. Her action had served two needs. "She knew her people would find you, knew you would lead them as you did, albeit with anger and poisoned thoughts but you guided them nonetheless as any god does. Xali is right, your people await. Rise to the status of the true gods you are, take the peace the Fates offer and leave this prison."

"He talks in riddles and lies," one of the gods said. As he spoke, his power leapt to Xali ready to attack.

Ren went to protect her, but then he saw the change in her. This time she was ready for it. He watched in amazement as she claimed the magic. Once again, it shifted around her in long waves like ripples that danced upon her skin. It wasn't hers to use as it would have been for Carnick, but it reacted to her power, drawn to it as a lover might be, controlled by it. She was one of their children whether they wanted to admit it or not. Their power would never be hers like it was Carnick's, but she held sway over it, and it reacted to her.

The water upon the ground glowed within the darkness, becoming brighter, and Ren could feel the Mother Fate's power that now ran through Xali's body. Had it always been there, below the surface waiting for her to claim it, or had it been granted to her with the immortality she now carried? His own power reacted to the sensation of it, his eyes changing as the specks in Xali's sparkled.

"You will have only one chance," Xali said, "she cannot turn the tide again, nor will she attempt to do so."

The closest god stepped to them, towering over them, the power almost too much for even Ren to bear.

"She turned her back on us, on me and everything I offered." There was anger in his voice, but it had softened, as though he were looking for her to continue to convince him that her offer was one to take.

"She loved another, nothing could have come between that, one tried but failed, only succeeding in getting us where we are today," Ren said, knowing instinctively that the god was talking of the Mother Fate. How had one woman, one Fate become so central to everything that had happened to his family, to him, to their world, to Xali and her family. All of it centering on her and her lover, and the brother whose jealousy had torn them apart. He remembered the stories his mother had told him, what she and his father had learned through the eons they'd walked the path of the prophecy. There had been so much that remained unknown yet there was enough to understand the depths of what she'd endured.

Xali extended her hand to the god. It seemed so small, she so miniscule and frail in comparison to them. This tiny girl was about to change the course of their world.

The god hesitated, looking back to his brothers. There seemed a consensus among them as one admitted, "I am tired of living below ground, brother."

The lead god looked at his hands, turning them over as if for the first time noticing they were not covered in a coat of tar and decaying lava. Then he looked back up at his brothers. "As am I."

As the words left his mouth, the god looked up, tilting his head, listening to something Ren couldn't hear, the other gods doing the same.

"Do you hear that, brother?" one to the side asked, Ren only now noticing the frail girl beside him, dressed in what looked to be a flowered gown. The skin below her gown was freckled with bruises. She was cowering, but her eyes were wide, staring at the god like she was seeing him for the first time. There was trepidation in her look along with fear, but also wonder. The silver hair that lined her head gave Ren no doubt this was one of Xali's cousins, one who'd lost her life, her soul now in the hands of the gods. Perhaps the one god beside whom she stood.

"It comes with understanding," the leader said, "and without hesitation."

Ren had no idea what it was they'd heard but whatever it was appeared to be swaying them. The god looked to Ren, those silver eyes appraising him once again, the red glimmers in them dancing as if they were lightning strikes. His brow furrowed.

"The Fates betrayed us, and you ask that we surrender ourselves to their wishes? That we accept this offering of peace?"

"They sent their creation here to you. I stand before you as proof of that offering."

"Do you? One who would be hard for us to kill now that your power has grown, now that you realize the true intent of it?"

"Yes. You can easily trap me here with you, my ability to shift is dampened here. I can fight you, but I am as trapped as you, as trapped as Xali. They sent me here to show that they are serious. There is a storm brewing above, however, and I would wager as Xali said, that you only have this one chance, this one moment. Whatever it is you heard, whatever it is that compels you to put aside the anger that has twisted your bodies and your minds since the day you were sentenced to this prison, listen to it now, or there will be no further chances at freedom."

The god nodded then looked back at his brothers once more.

"We all heard it, we are not forgotten, we remain," he said to them.

Then he turned back to Xali, taking her tiny hand in his. Ren let out the breath that had been sealed in his chest. For a moment, nothing happened, a strange silence falling upon them as the flames that licked the air above them slowly faded. Then the prison shook, the stone shifting, crumbling above them and all around. A rush of emerald water poured through an opening behind them, the cavern from whence it came collapsing. The surroundings creaked and groaned, the sound soon becoming thunderous until a power-ful rush of water flooded the prison, sweeping them all.

His hand grabbed for Xali's, but she was swept away before he could grab her. He couldn't shift, not wanting to leave her, and as he was pulled under, it was too late. Water muted the ability to shift, rendering it useless.

He was tossed within the current, all of them washed through the cavern in a tidal wave of power, rocks and debris pouring down upon them. He worried for Xali's safety as he searched for her. There was no way she could survive this, yet she'd survived the fall to this prison. His mind then reminded him that she now carried the same immortality as he.

His thoughts of her vanished as the echo of the crumbling mountain broke through. The entire mountain was coming down upon them. How were any of them to survive such a catastroph-ic event? Even with his immortality, was it possible? He prayed to his parents, prayed for Xali's safety, for Carnick's who was still somewhere on the mountain, for his own, as the water pushed him forward, clumps of rock pounding against him.

Carnick stared into the hole where Ren had disappeared. He'd been doing so since Ren had dropped through the weakened surface. He'd contemplated jumping in, but something had held him back. It wasn't fear. More like instinct. That this was not for him, that his part had been played. Sitting back, he sighed and looked around. They'd been fairly high up, and he had no ability to shift. He was stranded with no option but to walk back down. He didn't think he was meant to leave his spot, however. Something was happening, something that would change the course of it all; he sensed it deep within his soul. A type of knowledge that wasn't something physical, more like what Ren described as instinct. He stared at the sky, the storm still moving in above him, the snow having at least slowed to flurries. What was happening below him? Had Ren found Xali? Was she safe? Was she truly still alive?

Did the Fates know what it was that was happening there? Why Ren had fallen? Or were they as blind to it as he? He didn't think so, looking back at how the queen had come to him, urging him to look for Xali, telling him she was alive. No, with everything he'd learned about prophecy and the Fates, nothing was left unnoticed.

He rested his head in his hands, praying she was all right. It was a convoluted act now. He'd prayed to the gods his entire life. The Fates were foreign to him. His gods had given him power, immortality but they'd also been vengeful, destructive, the power changing him, possessing him. Until Xali's sacrifice. Since that moment, it had calmed, and he'd been more himself, the power that now ran through him one with what it had always been. It no longer seemed foreign to him; it was like a part of him that should have always been.

He thought of the god who'd appeared to him, directed him. Corrupted him. Had he always been that way? Had his gods always been so bent on revenge, on destruction? Or had they once been like the Fates? Was there a part of them that still was? Could one prayer help? Could it remind them of who they once were? Could it save Xali?

In that moment, he prayed. It was a prayer that was free of obligation, free of assumption, of a lifetime of being told those were his gods. He prayed in that moment, making a choice to believe that they were something more, that they were true and not corrupt as he'd known them. It was a selfless prayer and as he sent it, he felt at peace, sensing it had been the right choice to make.

He rested his back against the mountain and stared at the clouds, lost in thoughts of Xali until the ground below him began to tremble.

He scrambled up, watching as the trickle of emerald water that still dripped into the space where Ren had fallen, stopped, the drops pulling back, slowly moving upward, controlled by some unseen force. The droplets rose from the open space, making their way back up the mountain. Holding his breath, he waited. The mountain rumbled again, this time shaking with more force. He wobbled, grabbing the ledge for stability, backing closer, afraid of the fall even though he knew he was immortal.

The shaking continued, rocks crumbling from above the mountain, raining down upon him. A massive explosion echoed from below and then everything began to fall, his body with it. Debris pummeled him, his heart soaring to his throat as he began to free fall.

His mind remained on Xali. Was she down there? Underneath it all? Being crushed by the weight of the crumbling mountain? The mountain collapsed as if it had been hollow, and as he fell, he could suddenly see the ocean beyond, never having realized exactly how far up he'd been. He watched as waves crested violently between Xali's kingdom and the new land that had risen to connect the once distant island.

As the mountain fell, it crumbled into that space, the ground below the sea rising to meet it. His fall was nearly through, and he prayed the pain wouldn't be too extreme, prayed to his gods to keep Xali safe, to protect her. The land grew closer, uneven and littered with rock and pieces of the mountain. Closing his eyes, he braced for impact.

Pain and darkness. Flashes of light, more pain, his breath kicked back into his lungs, the healing of his immortal cells repairing quickly, yet not quick enough to keep him conscious. He blinked his eyes, knowing he'd been out for a short time. Rocks were crushed atop him, his breathing still labored as his cells fought the pressure.

He summoned his power and moved the stone, turning some of it to sand, heaving some aside until he could feel the air on his skin, see the gentle moon beams cutting through the dark clouds above. After taking a quick check of his body, relieved to find all of his parts still intact, he pulled himself up, scrambling from the pit where he lay, his mind back on Xali.

"Xali!" he screamed, running as steady and as fast as he could through the collapsed mountain. "Xali!"

Dust filled the air from the crash, making it difficult to see. He didn't have Xali's control of the wind nor the nature powers once looked upon as weak, so he had no way of parting it. Someone did, however. The air stirred, the dust and dirt clearing.

Ren was brushing himself off, looking around, his brows creased with concern. Xali was nowhere near him. Carnick ran to him.

"Where is she?" he yelled frantically.

"Fates, Carnick, you're all right," Ren said, grasping his arms.

"Where is Xali?"

Ren looked around. "I don't know. They were all right in front of me. Then…then everything exploded."

The smoke was still dissipating, but something in it caught Carnick's eyes. He stepped closer, a light moving toward him. The smoke thinned further, and he saw them, the gods. They'd changed physically, looking more similar now to the Fates he'd seen collect Ren's parents, but he felt the connection to his power. Instinctively, it called him.

They towered over Carnick and Ren, one stepping forward from the others, his hands holding something. His breath caught, a stabbing pain in his chest as the god opened his hands. Xali's body, looking fragile and small lay in them.

"No," he said, the world falling from under him.

The god morphed to Carnick's size, Xali now in his arms. Carnick felt Ren's hand on his shoulder.

"Give it a moment," he said with a tone that held too much optimism.

She's dead! he wanted to scream, but then she coughed, green water exiting her as the god lowered her to the ground. After a few more coughs, she drew a deep breath and swiftly moved to her feet, looking around wildly.

When she spotted Carnick, her eyes brightened, his heart leaping as they met his. She took a moment, evaluating him to make sure he'd returned to his former state, then she ran to him, throwing herself into his arms.

He held her tightly, reveling in the feel of her, the sensation of holding her once again, then moved back to look at her, touching her face, wiping away the tears that had left tracks through the dirt that stained it. Then he kissed her, ignoring all else but her and the need to kiss the woman he'd been torn from for moons.

She laughed as she returned his kiss.

"As joyful as this reunion is, I think we have other matters to address," Ren said.

Carnick pulled Xali to his side, instinctively tucking her behind him until she moved his arm and pushed herself back to his side.

"Immortal and powerful, Carnick," she said with a wink.

He was taken aback for a moment. She was immortal now? They both were? What did that mean for them? For this world?

She stepped forward, pulling his hand. He noticed Ren move as well. The gods were looking at their new circumstances, spreading out, delighting in their freedom.

"What happens now?" Ren said to the one who'd had Xali. "What will you do with your freedom?"

"We will bring this world to its knees—" one began.

The other raised his hand to silence him. "Our freedom was conditional, brother. In accepting Xaliandri's hand, I accepted those conditions for us."

There was grumbling from the others, the glow they carried dimming to a black haze that called to Carnick, his power surfacing.

"We may still have to contend with the Fates, but we now have a different course."

"We had a good course before they stole it all."

"Did we?" He turned to the others. "What did we have before the mortals, before the others cursed us to our prison? The mortals strengthened us, the prayers, the blessings, they were what kept us fed, kept us strong through the endless days."

"Are you saying we sit back and do what? Watch these people grow?"

"Our people, brother. They have been ours since the day the Fates banished them, and we found them. The girl is right. We have a purpose still, and now we have an heir." He turned to Carnick, pulling him away from Xali with his power. Carnick didn't fight it, instead continuing to stoically stare at the god.

"This one holds a part of us now. Before, we could only persuade their magic, but now we own it, we *are* his magic."

A silver glow appeared to Carnick's left, and the god released him.

"Orlaina," the god said in an eerie whisper.

The Mother Fate appeared, another male Fate with her. Aside from the silver haze that clung to them, they looked as Carnick and the others, taking a mortal form. They were both still difficult to look upon, his conscious knowing they held power beyond any understanding, just as the gods did. The silver shimmering upon their skin emphasized their beauty, a distinction to which even Xali's beauty paled in comparison.

"Aodhan," the god snarled, the others all drawing their power.

"Lower your power," the Mother Fate commanded. Orlaina, the god had called her.

Carnick marveled at the way her voice danced across his soul, making him lighter. He'd been stunned by her beauty the time they'd seen her in Ren's parent's quarters. She was breathtaking, ephemeral, eyes that rivaled the brightness of any star, emerald cascading around them, her long silver hair hung straight and thick down her back, sparkling in her magic.

The male was clearly a Dark Fate, his power swirling around him, the aura a contrast of his Darkness and her silver glow. His black hair and terrifying onyx eyes were a match to Ren's father's.

As powerful as the immortals were, Carnick knew these beings could snuff them out with ease. It was a strange feeling to know how miniscule he was in comparison to any of these beings. The Mother Fate walked toward the god, the Dark Fate remaining on guard. He wondered at their connection. Was this the lover they had spoken of? Or perhaps the brother?

"Fioch," she said, as she placed a hand on his, the other gods bracing, "my friend."

"I never wanted to be just your friend, Orlaina, and for that you let them imprison us. Let them steal everything from us, including you."

The air was growing thick with power. Carnick took a step back, his own power screaming for release. He moved cautiously away to stand next to Xali, noticing Ren was on his knees as if this was something one did in the presence of the Fates.

"Fioch, my heart was never yours to have. Diarmund has always owned it. Aodhan knew that," she looked back at the other Fate. "Although he was blind to it for a very long time."

"We all desire the one woman we cannot have, Fioch," the Dark Fate said.

So, this was not the lover but his brother, the one who had caused the trouble. No wonder the gods had reacted so in his presence. He had been the cause of their imprisonment, the impetus to everything.

"I was your friend, Fioch, I never promised more."

"Then why let them punish us? Punish me for wanting more?"

"Jealousy put you in that prison," the Dark Fate said, crossing his arms, "not Orlaina. She knew nothing of it." He sighed. "I convinced my brother that you were a threat. Once he was convinced, the others followed. We all protect Orlaina, and they all follow my command."

"I did not know until it was too late, until this world had become ours and grown populated with the first of our children. Then it was too late."

"But you did eventually free them," Xali said.

"Xali, don't," Ren said.

The Mother Fate turned to her, as did they all.

"You did so through me, through all of this, it was a means to an end, wasn't it?" Carnick could hear the anger in her voice and took her hand to hold her back. Snatching it away, she continued. "That's all this was? Why not free them yourself? Why drag us through this?"

The wind stirred, whipping around them, the sky turning black again. The Mother Fate lifted a brow.

"Orlaina, keep your child in check, or I will," the Dark Fate grumbled.

"The blood of curiosity will be the sacrifice demanded for your freedom," she said to Xali. "That was the seal placed on the prison. I could not free them, only you were chosen for that deed."

"Diarmund mumbled those words as we were sealed away," the god said.

"My brother, knowing Orlaina would seek your freedom and disavow herself from him without a way," the Dark Fate added.

"And that gave way for the addition to the prophecy," Ren said.

"Just like your father," the Mother Fate said to Ren before turning back to the gods, a glint of pride in her eyes. "I gave you a way out, and you took it. Do you still accept a place to rule alongside us? Your place in this world to continue as gods to my children?"

There was silence, and Carnick knew there would be no more answers to the questions that burned in all their minds. No more talk in front of them. This was a past that did not include anyone but the Fates and the gods. The only part they were meant to play, that of the prophecy, had been completed. The rest was not for their ears.

"You offer us your children?"

"Ones you claimed as my eyes were turned from them. They are no longer mine and Diarmund's, the others made sure of that." She shot the Dark Fate a look that would have toppled any mortal but only elicited a low feral growl.

The god she'd called Fioch, pushed her aside and came face to face with the Dark Fate. Both stared fiercely at the other, power eddying around them.

"She never would have been yours, Fioch, just as she has never been mine. It took me a very long time to see that, to accept it. Now I am only offering you this one chance to stand with us, join those who long for what my brother has and accept that your place is not by her side as his is, or you will be returned to your prison with no prophecy from Orlaina to help you the second time."

Fioch eyed him before turning back to the others. Some grumbled, others shrugged.

"Will there still be souls to torture?" one asked.

"You do what you will with your people," the Dark Fate answered. "Ours are off limits."

Xali gave a visible shudder, and Carnick wondered what she'd seen underground with them.

"Even the girl?"

Carnick protectively drew her to him, knowing exactly to whom they were referring.

"The girl is mine. Their child shall be yours but not her," the Mother Fate stated firmly.

"Child," Xali whispered, "so it's true."

"Shhh," Carnick said to her, the Mother Fate's words affirming Ren's suspicions. Xali must have figured it out on her own. He caught Ren's eyes, and Ren gave him a nod.

"What of our family?" Xali said suddenly.

"Xali, stop," he murmured, worried she'd upset the calm that had settled upon the space.

"Sartria and Ainia? The rest of them?"

"Sartria is mine," one said possessively.

Carnick couldn't help but wonder what had become of his cousin and the others. Xali seemed particularly concerned with Sartria, even after all she'd done to her, all she'd attempted to do with him. What had her punishment been that a god would claim her as his own? Had she finally been rewarded with a crown after all? The heavy crown of a god's concubine? He swallowed back the bile that rose at the thought. It seemed a fate worse than death, although death had already found her by his hand.

He glanced down at his hands, the memory of her neck snapping with his power still fresh, the blood stains he imagined layering his hands still visible in his mind. He had no doubt he would carry them through the eternity that now faced him.

"She is my family, and she deserves—"

"Nothing more than she has been given," the lead god, Fioch, interrupted, walking up to her and morphing back to his normal size. He towered over her petite frame, and Carnick worried for her safety.

"She deserves better," she said stoically.

"Their souls remain with us. Gaoth has claimed your cousin, and she will remain with him. The others, perhaps we'll think on allowing them freedom to move beyond. But that is all."

Xali looked as though she wanted to argue, but Carnick spoke up. "Thank you for the consideration. We humbly accept it."

It hurt him to say it, knowing that with the loss of her argument came the loss of bringing her parents' souls to rest as well as those of his parents. As much as he had hated his mother's ways, he still mourned her as Xali would continue to mourn her parents. As they would both continue to mourn all they had lost in the war that had been forced upon them.

The god's dark eyes studied him, brows knitting, and then he turned away from them, Carnick expelling the breath he was holding.

Fioch looked around then walked past the two Fates, breathing in loudly. "The air is fresh up here, the possibilities endless. We will accept, but we will take more land. You can give up this place where we have been imprisoned. You have enough of our stolen land."

"This range has always been part of Tenebron," Ren said defiantly, rising.

"Well, young one, it is no longer. You may be their mutt, but you do not control their land."

Ren dared look at the Dark Fate whose irritance with the god's request was palpable. He seemed like he wanted to argue again, but he stayed quiet. Carnick knew the insult hadn't set well either.

"Mind your place, chosen one," the Fate snarled as Ren tensed. Carnick heard the breath forced from him, noted the clench of his hands as he fought against whatever pain the Fate was inflicting. "You may have been gifted power, but that power can be stripped easily. Let that be a warning to all of you." Thunder rumbled above them, and the Fate looked to the sky. "Regardless of what your parents think," he mumbled, releasing his grip on Ren. He relaxed as Carnick felt the power recede, the air thinning. Ren was trying to catch his breath without showing it. "Fioch, you push your luck taking land from my people. My brothers will not be happy with this."

"How happy were my brothers when you stole it all from us? We will have the range."

With that, he turned and raised his hands out. The ground creaked and groaned as the collapsed mountain spread and lifted. The ground shook violently, and Carnick had no doubt the surface of their world was changing, the land ruled by him and Xali extending once again.

"You have connected more of the land than you did when you were fighting us. Your greed is reckless!" the Mother Fate yelled.

He snapped his head toward her, his eyes tinged with red. "And your ignorance of our demise was naïve, Orlaina. We will have this land. You will bless it with that nature gift of yours, and our people will thrive upon it. We claim the island space as well that we claimed during our battles. It will remain one piece of land, and you will not take it back."

Ren appeared to want to argue again, as though the island in the far distance, the one that now lie as one with the land, had once been important in his history, but he remained quiet. The Dark Fate grumbled something to Orlaina whose eyes looked sad.

"Fine but that is all. No more of my land will be yours. And you," he turned to face Carnick and Xali. "Your people will remain within their borders peacefully, or Drostiren will punish them. There will be no more upheavals from what is left of your damned family or your people."

"Do not threaten our pets," the god said to the Fate.

"You treat ours with so little respect as to insult him. I can threaten yours however I please."

They grew close again, chests protruding with anger, power spilling from them both, enough that it choked Carnick.

"If we are to live as one, we must respect all of our immortals, new and old," the Mother Fate said.

"I meant what I said, keep your people from our borders, or I will not hesitate to have them killed," the Dark Fate growled without looking from the god.

He didn't leave time for a rebuttal, disappearing in a flurry of silver and gold.

"Come home, my old friend," the Mother Fate said softly.

"To that welcoming?" the god said, the venom still clear in his response.

"It will take them time, as will it for all of us. Your place is with us."

The god walked over to Xali, pushing another god out of the way to reach her, and stared at her intensely. He was still in his enlarged state, making her appear as a child below him. "You would be wise to heed his warning, both of you. And keep that tongue in check. It's bound to get you into further trouble." He turned from her then nodded, throwing one last look at Xali, before muttering, "She has too much of your spirit, Orlaina. Did you do that to spite me?" He didn't give her time to answer before disappearing, his brothers following.

The god's words echoed through Xali's head. It swirled along with events she was still trying to contemplate. She wasn't certain how to comprehend it all. One moment, she had been fighting for her life trapped below a mountain prison, the next she was watching gods and Fates work out a feud that spanned the dawn of existence. She stared in disbelief at the space where the god had been, Carnick's arm tightening around her waist.

The Mother Fate remained as the others disappeared. Her eyes met Xali's, the emerald of them gleaming brightly. She glided toward Ren, taking his hands.

"There is much of your parents in you. Much of all of us, the final bonding of our journey, bringing my brothers and I together after all we struggled with. You have healed us, you and your parents. Now you will lead your people into a new era. It will not be easy, they have been through much, their numbers devastated, but under you and Paige, they will flourish once again, and the lands will return to what they once were. Stay strong and never doubt the love your parents have for you nor the place you hold in my heart."

She turned, gliding to Carnick and Xali, stopping momentarily in front of Carnick.

"You were once my children, and I was forced to send you away. Love created you, your ancestors pushed it away, forgetting me, but I never forgot you. A piece of me and Diarmund still resides within you even if you now favor the gods who claimed you in my absence."

She kissed his head, then moving to Xali, drawing her hand to Xali's cheek. A tingling sat where her hand touched, cool and calming.

"You are my child, as much as Violissa is, maybe more."

She brushed her fingers through Xali's hair.

"You are what was meant for your people. The strength and beauty. You have done well, changed the course of your world, the history of our land that had been forgotten." Tears glinted in her eyes. "I know it was hard. I was hard on Violissa as well. For that, I am truly sorry, but the hardships were necessary and now lay behind you. You are blessed and will remain so, Xaliandri."

Her fingers grazed Xali's face. "Stay true to who you are, who you always have been, my daughter."

She faded, the glimmer of silver in the air, the only reminder she'd been there. Xali stared at the space. They all stood in silence, no one knowing what to say, or where to go from here.

Ren finally made the first move. "I think that means it's over," he said, rubbing his arm and looking around.

"What does that mean for us?" Carnick asked.

"It means you're forgiven for being a cruel arse, and your wife is in your arms safe once more, no longer lost to us."

"You were quite a cruel *arse*." She emphasized the last word, using the term Ren and his people used.

Carnick looked bashful for a moment. "Xali, I'm so sorry, I never—"

"Shhh, you were not in control. You would never hurt me."

His eyes searched hers.

"Well, that's my cue to leave. I have my own wife whom I have not held in ages. I think two days' time is enough for you to reacquaint yourselves. Meet me in the northern keep as the rest seem to still be in shambles. Xali, I trust you can shift the both of you to—"

"To where?"

"Good question. Your palace is in worse shape than the remainder of ours. I'll leave that up to you. It's been interesting, let's try to avoid these intense situations going forward."

She laughed, and it felt wonderful. "Goodbye, Ren, and thank you."

He winked. "I'm looking forward to a long and hopefully uneventful reign alongside the two of you."

Then he was gone, leaving them alone on a land that now belonged to them. She looked back at Carnick meeting his stormy eyes. He appeared lost, and she realized she felt the same, unsure where to go next, what all of this meant, even what to say. So much had passed between them, could they ever return to the time of innocence they'd had before all of this had begun. Before their life had become filled with immortals and prophecy, gods and Fates?

Carnick reached out and tucked a stray strand of hair behind her ear, the sadness in his eyes tormenting her soul.

"I hurt you, Xali, something I swore I'd never do. I'll never forgive myself for what I did to you, to the others, the innocents… our child." His voice cracked, bringing tears to her eyes.

She took his hand and leaned her cheek into it, feeling the strength in it.

"None of it was truly you, Carnick, you were lost to me. And… and the child was never meant to be. He was a pawn, a means to an end. I sacrificed his life when I gave my own up for yours. You did not make that choice. That was on me."

He remained quiet for a few moments, and she gave him the silence.

"We had a child, Xali."

"No, Carnick. He was never ours. We will have a child. You heard the Mother Fate. We will still be blessed. I have mourned his loss, and I can do so no more, for if I do, I will not have the strength to move forward and greet our future child."

He drew her in and held her tight. She took in the familiarity of him, the strength, the smell that was distinctly Carnick, and she relaxed into him. His cheek lay upon her head, and in that moment, she never wanted to leave the safety of his arms again, all else could fade from existence as long as she had him.

"I missed you," she whispered.

She tipped her head up and met his lips, kissing him, giving herself over to him for the first time in moons. Desire washed through her as the strain of the past events fell away. Things would be all right; their mental wounds would heal just as their physical ones would.

"Let's go home," he said breathlessly.

"Where is that?"

"Wherever we make it," he answered, drawing back from her.

A memory of his vicious attack at their palace flickered in her mind, and she shivered instinctively.

"Someplace new," she said, "without the memories."

He took her hand and walked a little so that they were on a crest of what had been the mountains, the rest of the range stood to their right, towering well past their line of vision. The new land stretched before them, now part of the former holy lands yet distinctly different. Black sand glimmered with the remaining moonlight. The island the god had mentioned, now a part of their realm and hers to rule. She looked to Carnick who nodded.

Closing her eyes, she thought of that space that had once been the lone island, filled with some history that only Ren knew. She reached in under the nature to her Darkness and grabbed it, letting its power shift them to the land.

"Getting better at that, aren't you?" Carnick said, looking around. "What do you suppose was here before?"

"I don't know, but it meant something to Ren."

She leaned down and let the sand run through her fingers.

"Yes it did, something from his past."

"Or his parents'. Something was here once, I can feel it, like an essence."

She stood, looking out at the vast ocean beyond, then back at the land that lay before them. A land of hope, of history, of their people.

"Yes. We are not the same two people who started this journey, Carnick. It makes sense to start anew in the space that makes our land not the same land."

She spread her hand out, seeking any connection to it, to the possibility of vegetation. As if it had been waiting, sleeping until her claim on it, the land awoke. The sand remained in place but from below sprouted blooms and trees that grew at her command, heeding her call, reaching to please her. The world around them exploded in color.

She sensed a familiar presence in the air, one that matched her pull on the land and doubled it, the land coming to life, spreading far beyond to meet Gaernim, her realm. Streams bubbled from below the new growth, stretching to meet the river that ran through the rest of the land. As dawn broke, she stared out at the beauty that lay before them.

The gentle breeze lifted her hair, the calming touch of the queen.

Carnick took her hand. "Yes, I think this will be the perfect place to rule from."

She looked up at him, noting the violet specks that skimmed in his eyes, finally returned. Turning into him, she let her fingers dance through his silver hair then lost herself to his kiss, the touch she'd longed for over too long a period. As the world continued to flourish around them, so, too, did their love.

Seventeen

Ren stood, his hands behind his back, looking out of the same
window his father had once looked out. Things had been quiet, a calm in the air, a peace that had settled upon him since the
day they'd freed the gods. He'd needed it, peace had alluded them
for too long. He'd sent Cody and Thane to help Xali and Carnick
erect a new palace in the place they'd chosen to restart their life
together. Both men were eager to see Xali again, as it seemed a
bond had formed between the three on their trek together. He
shook his head, thinking of where the new capital of the Gaernim
realm now lie.

The Torathar island. It had played a significant role in the final steps of his parents' prophecy. Its very essence made from a
people who had been savagely annihilated by intruders. The first
people of this world. It seemed curious that the last of the world

were now living on land where the remnants of the first lay within the sand of its surface.

Perhaps, it was a coming full circle for the Fates. Perhaps, he was reading too much into it. He wondered momentarily if any power remained in its surface, the land lost to them, forgotten with the past. Torathar power had been purely Dark. Would any of it find its way to Xali? To Carnick? To their future child?

"Thinking too hard once again, son?"

Ren turned to see his father, looking the same as he always had aside from the sparkle of silver upon his Dark aura.

"Father."

"I would have thought with your tendencies, the Dark keep would be your last choice to stay."

Ren smiled. "Just a quick visit. It helps me think when I'm here, reminds me of you."

His father smiled. If he hadn't been Ren's father, the smile may have been terrifying, but Ren knew the man below and that the smile was sincere.

"You've done well, Drostiren."

Ren moved from the window to where his father stood.

"It's over, right?"

His father lifted his brow. "If it's one thing I've learned, it's to never grow complacent with the Fates."

"But you and Mother are among them now."

"Don't forget your uncle who has caused quite a stir with the others. He's a thorn in their side now instead of mine."

Ren couldn't help but laugh, knowing his uncle.

"It is safe to say the prophecy aspect of your life is now over. That does not mean that you or Xali and Carnick will not face obstacles, but as the Fates once told your mother and me, you are now adrift, as are they. Free to experience life without the constraints of prophecy."

Ren let that sink in, his very life the result of prophecy. "That's such a strange thought. Those words."

"Prophecy ruled our lives, and as so, it ruled yours. Do not let it do so anymore. You deserve a life free from its shadow. As does Xaliandri. Both of you have been shaped by it, your lives as much a part of it as the words themselves. You both are at the start of something new in our world, a world in which prophecy no longer guides it, one in which two very different rulers, three really, reign. Magic of the Fates now blended as before it has always ruled separately. This is your world now. We stand in the wings, here to guard and to guide, but it is you who are in control."

"And Xali?"

"Yes, trust me, she is being watched over. Your mother has taken a liking to her, and you know your mother."

Ren laughed. "Will I see you again? And Mother?"

There was a twinkle in his father's eyes. "You never know."

Ren grasped his father's arm to say goodbye, but his father pulled him in tightly.

"We will always be watching and always be with you."

"I love you, Father."

"And your mother and I love you. Now go lead this world as I taught you and stop this incessant worrying," he said, releasing Ren.

"Yes, Father."

His father disappeared, a silver dust shimmering where he'd stood.

Ren took a deep breath and shifted to the northern castle, throwing the doors of the meeting hall open. He nodded to his Council then to Xali and Carnick. He took a seat in his father's chair, watching as the others sat, Xali across from him at the other end of the table, Carnick by her side, she sitting where his mother had once sat.

It was time for the new era to begin.

Epilogue

Laughter filled the air, high and sweet. Xali tilted her head down, remiss to pull it from the sun's warmth, knowing she would soon be welcoming the night that lay in waiting. Vilana ran through the field, her silver braids shimmering in the sun's gaze, and Sintyne ran behind her, pushing roots from below to catch her.

"She's quick like her mother, and he never seems to learn that," Paige said with a wink, the blue of her eyes dazzling.

"Stubborn like her mother, too," Carnick said, sitting beside Xali who leaned against him.

"Stop relying on your nature powers, Sintyne," Ren called.

"And he is too much like his father," Paige said.

"Something that would stir the ire in my father," Ren returned.

"No, he would see it for what it is, the base to everything that makes him special."

They shared a moment, and Xali looked away to give them their privacy. It had been countless eons, too many for Xali's mind to grasp, but it had culminated in the two stars that frolicked before them, two future rulers, destined to love each other and to claim domain over their world. Xali wondered at the curiousness of it all as she fingered the necklace that had once belonged to her cousin and touched the smooth navy stone that still reminded her of the family they'd lost to the destiny that had led to this moment. No longer did prophecy play a part in their lives, yet the Fates had tied their children to one another just as they had once done to Ren's parents at the start of it all. She prayed it was not an ill-fated future, and in that moment, she felt the gentle touch of the breeze, that calm, the lilac that lingered. Her familiar guardian who had kept her word. Although she'd only known the queen a short time, she loved her dearly and had insisted her daughter bear the names of the two women who had shaped her life, the Fates that now watched over her daughter, Violissa and Orlaina.

"What are you thinking that would stir my mother's presence?" Ren asked.

She smiled. "Just thinking that my daughter needs to stop running and use her magic. I am not raising a damsel in distress."

"No such words have ever been muttered in your presence, my dear," Carnick said, kissing her head as he pulled her closer, his hand brushing the vines that still lined her arms, the loose shoulder of her dress exposing them.

As if she'd heard her mother, Vilana stopped, her eyes sparkling with flecks of emerald and violet that danced in the rising storm clouds.

The roots pushed away toward Sintyne, the ground rising below him to trip him from his unsteady feet. He fell, rubbing his head.

Ren shot Xali a look.

She shrugged. "Doesn't hurt him to realize my daughter is a formidable opponent. In fact, it would do him well to remember that."

"Aye, it would," he said, his lips curving to a sly grin.

She looked back as Vilana laughed and extended her hand to Sintyne to help him up. He reached for it then Xali felt the wind as Sintyne called it. Vilana was sent tumbling the other direction, the two remaining on the ground, bursting into a fit of giggles.

The future was now defined by the giggling children before them, ones who held the most powerful strands of magic their word had ever seen and would someday produce the one heir who would wield the power of both the Fates and the gods.

A shiver slipped down Xali's soul, and she prayed the combination would create a kind and steady ruler and not a mad man, a monster, the kind they all knew those powers could shape. Her prayer was answered with silence, no calming breeze or lilac, only the sound of giggles that floated on the breeze.

J. L. Jackola discovered her passion for writing in grade school when she wrote a short story that earned her a spot in a local writing workshop. She has been creating fantasy worlds ever since. When she's not weaving tales, she can be found logging miles in her running shoes, watching movies with her family, or curled up with a book. She resides in Delaware with her husband and three children.

To learn more, visit her website at www.jljackola.com.